DISCARD

The Eagle as Wide as the World

By X. J. Kennedy:

The Moonflower Stories:

The Owlstone Crown

The Eagle as Wide as the World

Uncle Switch: Loony Limericks
illustrated by John O'Brien

The Beasts of Bethlehem
illustrated by Michael McCurdy

Brats
illustrated by James Watts

Drat These Brats!
illustrated by James Watts

The Forgetful Wishing Well: Poems for Young People
illustrated by Monica Incisa

Fresh Brats
illustrated by James Watts

Ghastlies, Goops & Pincushions: Nonsense Verse
illustrated by Ron Barrett

*The Kite That Braved Old Orchard Beach: Year-Round
Poems for Young People*
illustrated by Marian Young

MARGARET K. McELDERRY BOOKS

X. J. Kennedy

The Eagle as Wide as the World

MARGARET K. McELDERRY BOOKS

MARGARET K. McELDERRY BOOKS

25 YEARS • 1972–1997

Margaret K. McElderry Books
An imprint of Simon & Schuster Children's Publishing Division
1230 Avenue of the Americas
New York, New York 10020

Book design by Angela Carlino
The text of this book is set in Perpetua.
Printed in the United States of America
First Edition

10 9 8 7 6 5 4 3 2 1

Library of Congress Cataloging-in-Publication Data:
Kennedy, X. J.
The eagle as wide as the world / X. J. Kennedy.
p. cm.
Summary: Continues the fantastic adventures of the twins Timothy and Verity as they attempt to
rescue their half-brother and save their land from a swarm of killer bees.
ISBN 0-689-81157-8 (alk. paper)
[1. Fantasy.] I. Title.
PZ7.K388Eag 1997
[Fic]—dc21
96-40458
CIP AC

For the kids who asked for more.
—X. J. K.

Contents

Thanks

Kate Kennedy, formerly an observer for the State of Arizona Bald Eagle Nest Watch, shared her knowledge of eagles and saved this story from several wild inaccuracies.

I am indebted to many writers, in particular to Sy Montgomery for facts about ladybugs, and to Sue Hubbell and John Crompton for lore and legends of bees.

After he read *The Owlstone Crown,* Teddy Ligon, a sixth grader in the Graham & Parks School, Cambridge, Massachusetts, suggested that Grandmother Tibb deserved to be made an Elder of the Land of the Moonflower too.

XJK

The Eagle as Wide as the World

1

Panic at a Picnic

A stiff breeze was doing its best to lift the corners of our red-and-white checked tablecloth. It kept trying to make Frisbies of our paper plates. I made a grab for a bag of potato chips so it didn't go sailing away.

Like the wind, I was uneasy, but I didn't know why. This was supposed to be our last chance to have fun. It was the day before my sister and I were supposed to start school, so we were having a picnic supper—just the three of us—on the side of Moonflower Mountain.

Naturally our younger brother was clowning, as usual. He was juggling a paper cup full of lemonade on the end of his nose. It fell, of course, splashing Verity.

"Mustard," said my twin sister grimly, "this picnic could do without you."

"What's a picnic without Mustard?" the kid shot back.

Ouch. That's Mustard for you. You see, his full name is Wildmustard Weedblossom. That's because he was born here in the Land of the Moonflower, where every kid is named after a plant. Maybe I ought to explain that Mustard is our half-brother, a year and a half younger than me and Verity. Actually, he's as good as a whole brother any day.

"That's a rotten crummy joke!" I shot at him, and whacked him with the bag of potato chips. The chips shattered, causing my sister to scream. Right away she threw me down on the grass with a cross-ankle pickup. Then she perched on my stomach and scowled down at me, her long brown hair blowing in the breeze, her eyes enormous behind her thick glass-doorknobby glasses.

"Squnching good potato chips!" she shrieked. "You ought to be ashamed of yourself, Timothy Tibb! I—don't—like—to—eat—crumbs!" She drove home every word with a knee-nudge in my ribs.

"All right, all right," I grunted. "Let me up, will you?"

"Say, 'Let me up, smart pretty Verity, my superior in every way.'"

"Let me up, smart pretty Verity, my—awww, do I have to say that?"

"Say it!"

I finished my recitation, gritting my teeth. "Now get off!"

Verity let me up, a victorious gleam behind her glasses. Even though she's legally blind, she can beat me up anytime she wants to. She used to be wrestling champ of Walter B. Pitkin Junior High back in Metal Horse, New Jersey. That was back when we lived on Earth, not Other Earth, where we live now. My sister is always giving me a hard time. She thinks she has a right to, just because she's twelve minutes older than me.

NOTE BY VERITY TIBB: *ME? Give TIMMY a hard time? I don't ever give him anything he doesn't deserve.*

You see? How she keeps butting in? Anything I say, she'll quibble with. No doubt she'll keep on poking her nose into this story. I'll be lucky to get in one word.

NOTE BY VERITY TIBB: *Well, it's MY story, too, after all. Timmy always blows up everything bigger than a circus tent. He never gets anything right.*

Defeated, I lay with my head on the grass, watching a stream of windmill moths skim down the mountainside, loaded with nectar from the Moonflower. The moths worked their wings like a pair of windmills going around. It was late afternoon, and up on top of the mountain the gigantic flower had just begun to open its bell-like blossoms for the night. By sunset, they would be open all the way, and people all over the country would breathe in the air and feel glad.

On my plate, a black ant was taking a hike across a crater of baked beans.

"Beat it," I told it. "Stop walking all over my supper."

"Excuse me," the ant's tiny voice piped. "Can't I have even one bean? You have so many of 'em."

I'll never get used to the animals talking. It surprises me every time.

"Oh, all right," I said. "Take your bean and go."

Carrying his burden, which was twice as big as himself, the ant staggered off into the grass.

Just as I was dumping myself some more lemonade, a cloud like purple smoke rolled over the sky and shadowed our tablecloth. Thunder started growling like a dog. Somehow the idea of being tickled by a lightning bolt didn't grab me. "Let's eat up," I urged, "and head home."

"Oh, for crying out loud, Timmy," said my sister, "what a yellow-bellied coward you are. A little thunder and rain won't hurt you. Aren't there any more watercress sandwiches?"

"You've had all four of 'em."

"Calling me greedy, are you? I ought to push your nose through your face and out the other side."

"Aaaah, you can't even see my nose," I said nastily. It was true, she couldn't, but after I'd said that, I felt a little bit guilty. Verity made a fresh lunge at me, which I managed to avoid.

Shivering in the breeze, listening to the thunder, I wished I was home in our house. I could see it in the distance, a mile away—the beautiful blue mansion on a ledge sticking out of the side of Moonflower Mountain. Our whole family lived there now. Only a few months ago, a dictator called Raoul Owlstone had made his headquarters on that very same ledge, but he and his army of stone owls aren't around anymore. Verity and I had made sure of that.

NOTE BY VERITY TIBB: *Us and some friends of ours, Timmy should have said.*

OK, OK, I've told about all that in a book called *The*

Owlstone Crown. If you haven't read it, that's all right. You can't read everything.

"Hey, you guys," said Mustard, "let's not fight, let's enjoy ourselves, huh? Your school starts tomorrow, remember? Two weeks earlier than mine."

"You *would* think of that," said Verity. "But maybe this new school won't be too bad."

"Want to bet? I've never been to a good school yet," said Mustard, rummaging the picnic basket and extracting a tuna sandwich and a brownie, which had squashed together. "All the schools make you do homework. And the teachers put you to sleep."

"Too bad you're too young to come to Hemlock School with us," said Verity. "Professor Hemlock is supposed to be interesting. Gramp says he knows everything there is to know about cubes and rectangles."

"Big deal. All I want to know about cubes is are there any ice cubes left? This lemonade's warm as bathwater."

For Verity and me, our fate was sealed. We were to set out for Hemlock School the very next morning. Our grandfather had heard it was the best school in the country. It was a long way from Moonflower Mountain, so my sister and I would have to live there all the time except for vacations. I dreaded the whole idea. I didn't want to leave Mustard and the mountainside and the Moonflower. Every time I thought about going off to a strange place, I felt all queasy, as if a squadron of butterflies had landed inside me, thrashing their wings.

"Cheer up, Timmy," said my sister, crunching an apple

with her two front teeth. "As soon as we've settled in, we'll have fun, right? They had better have a wrestling team. Hey, here's the sun again."

Sure enough, a blade of late sunlight had carved its way through the clouds. Parked on a clover, a bee started happily whirring its wings. That made Mustard think of something awful.

"Have you guys heard about killer bees?" he said gleefully, giving a big lopsided grin. "They're this big." With both hands he measured off ten inches of air. "They travel in swarms. I've read all about them. One time they ate a whole cow. And they stung a hole through six people."

"Mustard," said our sister, "if you don't quit talking yukky stuff like that, I'm going to beat you up."

But Mustard was just warming to his subject. His different-colored eyes, one green and one brown, shone gleefully. "And do you know what they do, those bees, when they attack a person? They start with the feet—chomp!—and they work their way up—chomp chomp! Hey. I don't believe this. Look at that bee. Holy smoke, you guys—look!"

Verity, of course, couldn't see much of anything. She said, "So there's a bee, so what? You've got bees on the brain. A little bee isn't going to hurt you."

Mustard was pointing at the sky. I looked up, and what I saw almost knocked me over. This was no ordinary honeybee—it was a giant bee with legs as long as fishing poles and two compound eyes like a couple of regulation basketballs. With an earsplitting drone it came roaring down out of the air, aiming straight at our tablecloth.

I grabbed Verity by the arm. "Duck, Sis! It's—it's a *monster!*"

Mustard had his camera out. "I want a picture of it!"

"Run, Mustard," I bawled. "For Pete's sake, run!"

But Mustard wouldn't budge. He was trying to focus his camera. Somehow I wasn't going anyplace either. Terrified, frozen to the spot, I watched that approaching bee.

The giant stopped, hovering right overhead, its legs working like the oars of a racing shell. It was so close that I could make out the three smaller eyes in its forehead, arranged in a triangle with the point pointing down, and the thick yellowish brown hair that covered its underbody. Its wings had panes like windows. A long whiplike tongue hung from between its chops, curled at its tip like one of those paper squawkers you blow out at a birthday party.

"Mustard!" I hollered. "Watch out!"

All of a sudden there wasn't just one bee buzzing down on us. A whole swarm of the things, every one of them six feet long, poured out of the sky.

Mustard's camera clicked, and the kid yipped, "*I got it!*" He tried to run, but the leading bee swooped down on him. Its two-pronged jaws picked him up like a crumb of food. Then, with our kid brother dangling and kicking his blue-and-white running shoes, the giant spun its wings like propellers and with a loud roar mounted the sky. Seconds later, the whole swarm followed. They darted over the mountain's crest. Dwindled. Were gone.

"Timmy! What's happened?" my sister wailed.

"They took Mustard," I said dully. "Those giant bees have carried him away."

I stared at our pathetic picnic, what was left of it. The pickle jar, knocked over on its side, was drooling green juice all over the crumpled tablecloth.

2

Impossible Demands

Deep in thought, the Land of the Moonflower's number one detective paced the top of our grandfather's desk. His bright red back, with its seven black polka dots, moved slowly north, then did a U-turn and headed south. Within his head, which was no bigger than a grain of sand, his keen mind must have been racing.

"Rats!" he exploded, coming to a halt. His voice was small and rasping. "Why would anybody grab the kid? How come they didn't ask for ransom? This whole case smells like a bucket of secondhand fish."

Right away, when Verity and I had burst into Gramp's office in the blue mansion, gasping, "Mustard—he's been kidnapped!"—Gramp had acted. He had stuck his head out of the window and shouted up into the blossoms of the Moonflower, "Lew! Come down here, will you?" And in seconds, Lewis O. Ladybug was on the job.

Even though he was only a little ladybug like any you'd see on a rosebush, Lew was as smart as Sherlock Holmes. Right now, he flew up and perched on the collar of my shirt to question me.

"So what did those oversize bees look like?"

"Lew, they were fantastic! They were unbelievable! They were stupendous big! They—"

"Quit flapping your chops, junior. Exactly *how* big were they?"

"Biggest old bees you ever saw. Six feet long, thick as an oak tree. They had eyes the size of watermelons."

The detective glared. "Since when do bees come that big? If you're making things up, you'd better watch it. I'll feed your teeth to you."

At that threat, Gramp looked shocked, but I was used to Lew's tough way of talking. He was always trying to make up for his small size. Really, he's the best friend I've ever had, not counting Verity.

My sister backed up my story. "Timmy's telling the truth, Lew. I couldn't see those bees too well, of course, but they were monsters. Big enough to carry off Mustard, all right."

"OK, I believe you. Now what kind of bees were they? Hornets, wasps, bumblebees—which?"

"I—I'm not sure," I said.

"Think, junior. Work your head. Did they have stripes?"

All of a sudden—wow! I remembered Mustard's camera. Just before the big bee had whisked him away, the kid had snapped a picture of it.

"Lew, we've got a photo of one of 'em! Mustard took it. We just need to develop it."

Sure enough, Mustard's camera was still in the picnic basket where he had tossed it before he was grabbed. I removed the film and, at a whistle from Lew, a windmill moth swooped in and picked up the roll and bore it away to the police photo lab, while Lew bawled, "I want *big* prints! Glossies! And step on it!"

Gramp had sounded an alarm, and now our whole family had assembled. Our grandmother, who'd been out in the garden painting a picture of our mother, appeared in her paint-spattered smock, tucking a stray lock of salt-and-pepper hair up under the band around her head. Mother had a daisy in her hair. Gosh, how she reminded me of Mustard. Reddish, mustard-colored hair. One green eye and one brown. Thin, pale Dr. Weedblossom had come running, too, out of breath, his horn-rimmed glasses parked on his forehead. He's our stepfather, a real good guy—the inventor who'd met and married Mother in Moonflower Land.

Everybody made a circle around us and Gramp. Verity and I had to retell our story from the beginning, with my sister putting in corrections along the way.

NOTE BY VERITY: *Well, Tim was blowing things up as usual. There couldn't have been a MILLION bees. A hundred, maybe.*

When Mother and Dr. Weedblossom learned that their son had been kidnapped, Mother let out a shriek and had to sit down on a chair, and the doc did his best to comfort her.

Gran was hopping mad. With her ferocious, big-eyed look, she was somebody no kidnapper would want to meet.

"This is an outrage!" Gran shrilled. "Agamemnon, you and I are Elders in this country and you're Eldest Elder. Can't you find out where the boy has been taken to?"

It was true—Gramp was the closest thing to a president that the Land of the Moonflower had. And not long ago, all the people in the country had elected our grandmother one of the Elders too.

"Now Agatha," said our grandfather, "you know I'll do everything in my power. That's why I've called in Lewis Ladybug."

Gran turned to the detective. "Lew, what do you think? What will those terrible creatures do with Wildmustard?"

"Don't worry your head, Mrs. Elder Duff," said Lew. "I bet they'll treat the kid first-class. After all, he's valuable to them."

"How do you mean?"

"Well you can bet your bottom buck that they're going to want a whale of a ransom for him."

Gramp ran a restless hand through his sparkling white hair. "I don't get it, Lew. Why weren't Tim and Verity kidnapped too? Why did those rascals seize only Wildmustard?"

"I'm just guessing, Elder Duff, but I'd say those bees were programmed. They were supposed to snatch only one hostage, so that's what they did."

"This is perfectly dreadful," said our mother. "I want

to know, Lewis Ladybug, what you propose to do about it."

"What do you think I want to do, lady?" said Lew, glowering. "Find the kid is what. For a start, I'm ordering my cousins to comb the land. I've got plenty of cousins—the beetles. Half a million of 'em, and they don't miss anything. Besides, I'm putting twenty of my best wind-mill moths on the job. They'll look under every stick and stone."

"After all," Dr. Weedblossom put in, "if those giant bees have a nest or a hive—and what bees don't?—it must be a half a mile wide."

Me, I was remembering Mustard, his cockeyed grin, his mustard-colored hair, his different-colored eyes, and I could just imagine the younger kid before me. I wondered what it had felt like to get carried away in the jaws of a giant bee. Me, I'd have been scared silly.

"The fact that those bees were giants," Dr. Weedblossom said thoughtfully, "may tell us something. They could very well have come from April Fool Isle."

"Where's that?" Gramp wanted to know.

"In the Gulf Stream, perhaps five hundred miles from here. Its animals are said to be giants. Explorers have found evidence of a great bird that the natives call 'the eagle as wide as the world.' Just how large it really is, the explorers couldn't say."

"Why not?" asked Lew.

"Because they couldn't see it. The eagle is invisible. All the explorers saw were her tracks—and some enormous eggs."

An unseeable giant eagle! Another one of a zillion odd

things Dr. Weedblossom knew. That was interesting to hear about, but at the time, I couldn't imagine how that fact was going to help find Mustard. At the time, that is. Who could have guessed that in a little while—

NOTE BY VERITY: *Timmy, slow down! You're getting ahead of the story. Just tell what happened, one thing at a time.*

Just then, there was a knocking at the window. Mother opened it and a large black bird came flapping in—a crow with a little metal can strapped to one leg. This character perched importantly on Gramp's desk, gave a caw, and cried, "Attention! A message from Her Majesty the Queen!"

The messenger let Gramp open the metal can and take out a small, folded piece of paper—gray, like the nest of a wasp. Gramp smoothed out its wrinkles and read it to himself, looking serious.

"Where did you get this?" Gramp demanded of the crow. "Who gave it to you?"

"A bee did. One of those big ones. Said if I'd bring it to you I'd get a whole bushel of corn."

Lew Ladybug spiraled up from the desk and perched on top of the crow's beak. Squaring his strong biting jaw, he looked the messenger in the eye and rasped, "So where's that big bee now? Where do you collect your payoff?"

"Won't tell," said the crow. "Said if I told you, I wouldn't get paid, I'd get stung. Now get off my beak, you puny buglet, before I munch you up."

Lew leaped aside, just in time to avoid a snap of the beak. He barked, "Try that again, buster, and you'll eat some knuckle sandwiches. For two cents I'd pull your tail out through that smart-talking beak of yours. Elder Duff, let's throw this flapping rat in the cooler. Hold him there till he squeals."

I made a jump for the window, but the crow was too quick for me. Before I could cut off his escape route, the messenger gave one last jeering caw and flapped away.

"Gramp, what does the paper say?" Verity wanted to know.

Our grandfather adjusted his glasses and read aloud:

"To Eldest Elder Agamemnon Duff:
Your grandson is my hostage. He will be held until you meet the following demands.
First, you will notify all insects in this country that from now on they are denied access to the Moon-flower.
Second, you will allow only my bees to collect its pollen and juice.
Comply at once!
From the royal hand of Her Majesty
Meadea, Queen of the Bees"

"What a mean queen!" said my sister. "Lew, where does she live? Wherever it is, maybe that's where she's holding Mustard."

"Beats me," said the detective. "I don't know anybody in this country named Queen Meadea."

"This is good news!" said Gran cheerily. "Wildmustard is alive and safe! Now, Agamemnon, surely we can let those pesky bees drink from the Moonflower, can't we? What's the harm?"

"The problem," said Gramp thoughtfully, "would be to keep out the other insects. I can't do that. Why, without Moonflower nectar, all the ants, moths, and little bees would die."

"And ladybugs," added Lew.

"They'd all die and so would the whole land. Our flowers and plants need pollination. The Moonflower can't belong to one colony of bees alone. It is for all."

"Lew," I begged, "let me help find Mustard."

"Nah, kid," said the detective. "You don't have as many eye cells as a beetle. Besides, there aren't as many of you. Anyway, aren't you supposed to go to school tomorrow morning?"

My heart sank. In the excitement, I'd managed to forget about that.

Gramp said, "That's right, Timothy. You and Verity must go to Hemlock School just as we've planned."

"Aw, Gramp—"

"Cool it, junior," said the ladybug. "Do like your granddad says."

Verity had been simmering like a kettle. Now she blew up. "Gramp, you don't really expect us to start school tomorrow, do you? With Mustard kidnapped and everything?"

But Gramp wasn't changing his mind. "I certainly do, my dear. Here at home, you're in danger. But Hemlock School is far away, and the kidnappers won't look for you there."

My sister looked ready to cry. "I can't go to school—I just can't! How am I supposed to concentrate on geometry and geography and geology and all that geo-stuff? I'm so worried about Mustard, I can't think!"

Gran wrapped an arm around her gently. "You're upset, child. We're all upset, but let's try not to worry. When Lewis starts his investigation, those bees had better watch out. And Verity, aren't you forgetting Shelley Snail? Why not take it to school with you?"

Verity lit up like a switched-on light. She clapped her hands and gave Gran a hug. "I forgot about Shelley! Listen, everybody, and I'll ask it to predict!"

And she fished in the back pocket of her jeans and brought out a little round shell, as yellowish as a piece of old ivory. It was Percy-Mary Bysshe-Wollstonecraft Shelley Snail, poet and prophet—Shelley for short. You call a snail "it" because it isn't either a girl or a boy. It was amazing. You could ask it any question about the future and it would answer you, even though you couldn't always tell what the answer meant.

The snail's tiny mouth opened and a shrill voice came out, pausing after each word:

"You. Want. Me?"

"Shelley, you've got to help us," pleaded Verity. "Mustard has been kidnapped by giant bees. What will happen now?"

In the palm of her hand, the snail drew back into its shell until we could see only its two bright pointy eyes on stalks, wavering. Minutes dragged by, as the snail searched the future. Finally its head reappeared. There was a hush in the room as it spoke:

17

"He. Whom. Bees. Snatched. Now. Labors. For. A. Queen. Those. Who. Would. Rescue. Him. Must. Walk. Unseen. At. School. Within. Their. Breakfast. Bread. These. Two. Shall. Meet. A. Comrade. Who. Reveals. A. Clue."

Lew gave a twitter of annoyance. "Snail, your prophecies are about as clear as Mississippi mud. What's this stuff about walking unseen? 'These Two'—that's Verity and Tim, all right, but what has bread got to do with anything?"

"Don't. Ask. Me," said the snail. "I. Just. Foretell. The. Future. I. Don't. Explain. It."

But I felt hopeful. Maybe Verity and I could help track down the kidnappers after all. I promised myself to take a good close look at my breakfast toast.

Just then came a tap at the windowpane. The windmill moth had arrived with the finished pictures. The whole family crowded around Gramp's desk. Gramp shuffled through the snapshots, setting aside all the ones Mustard had taken of himself making funny faces, and held up the last shot on the roll. It showed a yellowish brown bee with black stripes around its body, seen from the ground looking up.

"OK, they're honeybees," said the detective. "This narrows the search."

"Agamemnon," said Gran to Gramp, "even in school these children will need protection, won't they?"

"Yeah, Elder Duff," said Lew, "how about sending your grandkids to school with a bodyguard?"

"Send Fardels Bear," pleaded Verity. "He's the best, strongest bodyguard in the world."

"That's who," Lew agreed. "Fardels is the man for the job, you might say."

Gramp nodded approval, and I felt cheerful. Fardels is a Kodiak brown bear standing ten feet tall and weighing a thousand pounds.

Another bright idea hit me. "And, Gramp, can we go to school in the little blue blimp?"

"Why not?" said our grandfather. "I was planning to take you there myself, but now I must deal with this crisis. You and Verity and Fardels had better leave at dawn, so that you'll get to school on time. Now it's late. Off to bed with you!"

Tired out from excitement, I gladly crawled in between the sheets, but do you think I could sleep? No way. Every time I started sliding into dreams I'd wake up again. I kept thinking about poor Mustard hanging from the jaws of that monster bee, carried off to—where? What had this Queen Meadea done with him? Verity and I just *had* to find that clue, as the snail had foretold.

For the first time in my life, I could hardly wait for summer vacation to be over.

3

Airborne with a Bear

Dawn. The climbing sun was spraying gold on the dark underbellies of the clouds. I pushed the starter, and the little blue blimp's engine purred to life. Soon its propeller was whacking the air like a big floppy-bladed electric fan. Our takeoff wasn't easy. The engine strained, the cabin creaked and groaned. After all, we had a thousand-pound Kodiak Alaskan brown bear on board.

Carefully, I steered the little aircraft out of its hangar beside our house and tugged the stick back, and the blimp lifted its light blue nose and climbed ever so slowly over the trees. I aimed the nose sharply higher and we rose—up, up, past the Moonflower itself. Rooted atop its mountain, the big plant still had its blossoms open wide. Pretty soon, as the sun rose, it would close them for the day, but right now in earliest morning they loaded the air with a tangy perfume and a gentle, silvery light.

When the altimeter said five hundred feet, we leveled off, and the blimp settled into a steady course. The blimp's engine wasn't much bigger than a motorboat's, but it sure made plenty of noise. Inside the wooden cabin attached to the little airship's underside, everything rattled and shook so hard that we had to shout to make ourselves heard.

I loved to pilot that little blue blimp—loved to, better than anything. Dr. Weedblossom had built it for me for a birthday present. It was a neat invention—it didn't need helium gas to make it float, it used ordinary air. Anybody could drive it. It was as easy to steer as a tricycle. You shoved the joystick to the left or right, and under the blimp's tail a rudder would turn. When you wanted to go up or down, you pushed the stick forward or drew back on it, and a fin on the blimp's tail would tilt in the right direction.

Sometimes I'd let Verity take a turn at the joystick, even though she couldn't see where she was going. Of course, I had to give her a little advice so that she didn't hit anything.

NOTE BY VERITY: *Huh! Timmy isn't telling about the time he slammed the blimp into Farmer Elderberry's barn. I didn't have a thing to do with THAT.*

Well, nobody's perfect. But even if you *did* hit something, you didn't get killed, because the blimp was as light and slow-moving as a cloud.

Despite the early hour, our whole family had turned out to see us off. Everybody except for the missing Mustard. Mother and Gran were there, squeezing the breath out of us and telling us to get plenty of sleep and not miss any meals and everything. Lew Ladybug stopped by and told us to keep our noses clean. He promised he'd drop in on Hemlock School sometime and check up on us.

Gramp gave our bodyguard some last-minute orders. "Remember, Fardels, don't let Tim and Verity out of your sight any longer than you must." To which the bear replied that Gramp didn't need to worry; if anyone lifted a finger to hurt us, he'd slap them down. Gramp promised to send us news about the search for Mustard, and he shook hands and told us to study hard, especially in his favorite subjects, which were philosophy and boat-building. Dr. Weedblossom for a going-away present gave us each a new watch, his own invention. It told you what time it was on every planet in the solar system, in case you needed to know.

From the copilot's seat beside me, Verity yelled louder than the engine noise, "Timmy, how long will it take Lew to find Mustard?"

"He'll work fast. Him and his millions of cousins."

"I think it's mean of Gramp to send us to school at a time like this."

"Gramp isn't mean," I shouted. "He's only trying to do what's best, you know. Anyhow, this is one time I don't mind going to school. Didn't Shelley say we'll find a clue?"

"Ummm, yes. Something about bread." She patted her back pocket, making sure the little poet and prophet was still there.

A chomping noise was coming from behind me. Our bodyguard was holding half of a cherry pie in his paws.

Red filling dripped down and matted the hairs under his chin. Now he was licking off his claws, which looked like yellowish white Brazil nuts. He rumbled, "Hey, nice of your mother to send this snack along."

"Fardels, you slob," I told him, "quit dripping. Save that other pie for me and Verity, will you?"

I really liked Fardels, you understand. He had a face you could trust. Deep-set eyes, sloping forehead, little, rounded ears, and that short stiff beard full of pie guck. Maybe he was a mess right now, but it felt good to have him along.

Through the pilot's window, I could see that fall was coming on. Here and there, the leaves of the maples had started turning red and gold. The Land of the Moon-flower was mostly forests and farms. It wasn't much on factories because nobody had invented cars, radios, television sets, computers, movie projectors, phonographs, VCRs, camcorders, or anything like that. You might think that without all those things the country would be pretty boring, but somehow, with lots of books and sports, we always found plenty to do.

I steered south, and we purred along toward Hemlock School. Dr. Weedblossom had put an X on a map for me, showing its whereabouts. The sun blazed. The trip was long, but Fardels gave me a rest. He took a turn at the controls, growling out of his window at any high-flying moths and birds: "Hey, you—out of the way!"

About noon, I eased the blimp down into a clover field, where we broke open the sandwiches and the pie that Fardels had spared. Then we sprawled on our backs in the grass and smelled the big ripe clover blossoms. Bees—little harmless ones—were landing on them and taking off again. For a while, I almost forgot to worry about Mustard.

We stayed too long. By the time we were in the air again and back on our way, the sun was sinking. Uh-oh—we were supposed to report to school by three o'clock!

It was practically dark when at last the red brick bulk of Hemlock School rose out of the trees. I circled, deciding where to land. The school was one building with tall chimneys. There didn't seem to be anything else on the premises, except for a barn and a shed and a few heaps of brick and metal out in back, as if something had been torn down lately. Beds of bright blue and yellow flowers surrounded the building. In front of it stretched a broad, flat, empty plaza—a pretty good landing space.

I threw the joystick forward and nosed the blimp down, down, down, until the bottom of our cabin scraped the ground. Fardels threw open the door and flung out the anchor, a sack of cement on the end of a rope. I killed the engine, and the little blue blimp settled happily into its parking space, like a boat at anchor bobbing in the breeze.

Fardels tossed out our bags, and I jumped down, followed by Verity. The bear hit the ground with a thump, like the half ton that he was.

"You are late," came a woman's shrill, grating voice. It reminded me of a piece of chalk squeaking against a blackboard.

The woman had on a hairy-looking tweed skirt and a

blouse full of ruffles. Her paste-pale face had a sharp, pointed nose and wire-rimmed glasses. The glasses stayed on her nose by pinching it. The nose tilted skyward, as if sniffing something she didn't like. Her thin lips were fixed in a straight line, which never went up at the corners. Evidently the woman wasn't much given to smiling. Behind her was another, shorter person, a youngish man who walked slightly stooped over.

I started to stammer an excuse, but Verity butted in: "We're sorry, Professor Hemlock, honest we are. We completely lost track of the time."

"Are you blind, girl?" said the squeaky woman in irritation. "I am not a man—I am Mademoiselle Stinger, assistant to Professor Drone, your headmaster. No doubt you tardy brats are the Tibb twins. Well, I must say, you've begun school badly. From now on you will keep this lesson in mind: *At Sweetness and Light Academy, we are punctual.*" She was holding a stick ruler, and all the while she spoke she kept slapping the palm of her hand with it.

"Professor *Drone?*" I echoed. "Who's he? Sweetness and—what? Isn't this Hemlock School?"

"This *used* to be Hemlock School," snapped the mademoiselle. "Now it is under new management."

"What's happened to Professor Hemlock?" Verity asked.

Mademoiselle Stinger's voice grew even more shrill. "Impertinent brat. That is none of your business. And how dare you bring that filthy beast to school with you? We allow no pets. Especially not"—and she shook with loathing—"a *bear.*"

"What have you got against bears?" Fardels wanted to know.

"I detest bears! Bears are thieves. They break into hives and steal honey from the honest, hardworking bees. Bear, I shall have you destroyed!"

4

Noises in the Night

Verity balked.

"No way!" declared my sister. "Nobody's going to destroy Fardels. We're not setting foot in this place. This isn't the same good school it used to be. Come on, Timmy, come on, Fardels, let's go home!"

But Mademoiselle Stinger wouldn't hear of that. "Ben Ivy!" she squeaked to the stooped-over young man behind her. "Deflate that aircraft!"

Her servant seemed unwilling. "But it's such a neat little blimp."

"Silence!" cried Mademoiselle Stinger. "Do as you're told, you hunchbacked toad! At once!"

Ben Ivy—I noticed now that he'd been born with a handicap, a thick back that caused him to stoop slightly—threw me a glance that seemed to say, "I'm sorry, truly I am." He took two reluctant steps forward, and of course he ran up against Fardels. Fardels gave a growl. Ben Ivy backed away. I didn't blame him a bit.

"Obey me, Ivy!" screeched the mademoiselle. And she lifted her stick ruler to crack her servant's head.

But the brown bear didn't approve. A roar rumbled out of him. His paws caught the mademoiselle's hand and twisted it. Her ruler dropped to the ground. Ben Ivy flashed a grin of gratitude.

Mademoiselle Stinger was seething. Her bulbous eyes flashed. "Filthy brute!" she spat.

Fardels arched his back and showed his teeth. "Who are you calling a brute?" he wanted to know.

"This is no brute," said my sister. "He's chief zookeeper of Moonflower Land. And he's our bodyguard."

"I shall have him made into a rug," said the mademoiselle coldly.

"But our grandfather sent him with us," Verity insisted. "To protect us. You see, our little brother has been kidnapped by some giant bees. Gramp doesn't want that to happen to us too."

"Pish, posh, and piffle, you silly goose," said Mademoiselle Stinger. "You'll be perfectly safe here at Sweetness and Light Academy. Why, we have our very own police force."

"Just the same," I put in, "Fardels is supposed to guard us. Gramp told him to."

The mademoiselle sighed. "Your grandfather, the Eldest Elder—does he expect this vile brute to stay with you?"

"That's right," I said. "You can ask Gramp for your-self."

"Oh, very well," said the mademoiselle reluctantly, but I could tell she was mad as a wasp. "You may keep your bear. But if he crosses me once more . . . !"

"I told you—we're not staying!" Verity cried.

"Listen, Sis," I whispered to her, "maybe we *ought* to stay."

"Are you goofy, Timothy Tibb?"

"Remember what Shelley predicted? If we stay here in school, we'll pick up a clue."

Verity remembered. She swallowed hard. "Oh, all right," she said out loud. "We'll stay—for a while. But we want to keep the little blue blimp. And Fardels stays with us too!"

"The bear," said Mademoiselle Stinger evenly, "will sleep out in the barn with the cows."

Fardels growled. "Oh no I won't. Cows are no fun. All they can talk about is grass. Anyhow, out in the barn I'd be too far from these kids. I've got my orders—I'm to stick close to them at all times."

"What about it, Miss Stinger?" chimed in Verity. "Can't you find room for Fardels in the boys' dorm?"

The assistant kept drilling us with her steely glare. "Brute, you must sit in the last row of every class and keep perfectly still. If you cause the slightest disturbance, I shall send you packing."

"Don't worry," said Fardels gruffly, "I'll keep mum as a mouse."

"As for your sleeping quarters," mused the headmaster's

assistant, "it offends me to lodge a beast such as you in this school building. This is most unusual. However, because the twins are Elders' grandchildren, we shall make an exception. Boy, you and the bear will share a room. But, bear, don't you dare eat any honey in your bed and drip all over the bedsheets, or—out you go!"

Ben Ivy stepped forward to carry our bags, but Fardels waved him away. The bear stood up on shaggy hind legs and with one powerful paw hoisted all our stuff—even Verity's bag of weights for lifting. Verity always has to struggle to budge those weights, but the bear picked them up like a bundle of feathers.

"What's that clanking stuff?" squeaked the mademoiselle. Verity explained about the weights. How she lifted them every day to build up her wrestling muscles.

"Well you won't need those things here," said the assistant with a sniff. "We allow no sports at Sweetness and Light Academy."

"No sports?" cried my sister in disbelief. "How can you—why not, for Pete's sake?"

"Professor Drone permits no idle games."

Verity looked sad. Fardels gave a shrug and tossed the weights back into the blimp.

"Follow me," said the mademoiselle curtly. "Ben Ivy, back to the basement, you swine, and do the laundry."

Did I really want to attend Sweetness and Light Academy? I could imagine all the kids back home teasing me when they heard that name. The school wouldn't even have any basketball team. I didn't like Mademoiselle Stinger. Her cold, beady stare never changed, and her squeaky-chalk voice set my teeth on edge. Professor Hemlock, the old headmaster—what had become of him?

Trailing after the mademoiselle, we hiked through a half mile of hallways, up and down stairs, and stopped briefly at a supply closet, where she dug us out some school uniforms.

As we were climbing a long, wide staircase to the second floor, three very strange figures were coming down. They wore bright green robes with hoods pulled low. All I could see of their faces were their shiny eyes. There was something mighty odd about these figures. As they glided by us, I thought I heard a buzzing sound.

"Those are the Hoods," said the assistant, noticing my quizzical look. "Our school police. They have orders to arrest any foolish student who tries to run away."

"Why," said Verity, who always told the truth, even when she shouldn't, "that's exactly what *I* want to do."

Mademoiselle Stinger gave a sniff. "You'd be sorry. The last student who ran away . . ." Her sentence trailed off, as if the poor student's fate had been too horrible for words.

"Timmy," said my sister under her breath, "this isn't a school—it's a jail."

Verity's room had one square window, with a view of a brick chimney. There was a narrow bed and a dresser shaped like a cube. No pictures, no rugs, no anything to make you feel at home. A lonesome beeswax candle guttered in a holder on a wall.

"Brrrr-r-r-r!" said Verity, giving a shiver, "what a cold-looking place!"

Stinger sniffed. "It's good enough for you, Mistress Tibb. Breakfast will be served at six-fifteen. You will hear a buzzer. You will then report promptly to the cafeteria downstairs, showered and dressed in your uniform. Understand?"

"Oh, perfectly," said Verity.

"When's dinner tonight?" asked Fardels, licking his lips.

"Dinner was at five o'clock. It is now six. You greedy brute, you'll get no more food today."

All of a sudden a loud, muffled boom shook the floor and rattled the window.

"Don't be alarmed," said the mademoiselle quickly. "It is nothing. Professor Drone must be blowing up something again."

Then she gave Verity a last cold stare. "Let me warn you, young mistress, that whenever you are not in class or at a meal, you will remain inside your room. You may walk as far as the bathroom down the hall—no farther. Do not visit, do not roam the halls, do not—I repeat, *do not*—snoop into anything not your concern. After lights-out, you may not leave your room for any reason. Good evening!"

My room on the boys' floor, another flight up, was as grim as Verity's. The only difference was that it had *two* beds—old rickety things that jingled when you sat on them—and a teetery chair. Stinger went away, after more warnings.

The bear and I settled in. Fardels was staring in puzzlement at his school uniform, a shirt and pants, yellowish brown with broad black stripes.

"How am I supposed to get into this monkey suit?" the bear wondered. "These pants wouldn't fit a cub." The shirt, too, proved too small for him. He managed to struggle into it, but when he took a breath it split down the back with a loud *ripp-pp-pp!*

"Fardels, you must be the fattest student they have," I said, laughing. I crammed my clothes into the dresser, and my photo collection. Fardels opened his leather sack and hauled out a speckled trout. He flopped himself down on his bed—his weight almost bent the creaky thing double—and began chomping on the fish, starting with the head.

"Want some?" he invited, mouth full.

"No thanks. Didn't the mademoiselle say not to eat in bed?"

"She only mentioned honey. Didn't say a thing about fish."

The fishtail vanished. The bear wiped crumbs from his beard, lay back, and soon was snoring.

Despite Fardels's fondness for smelly fish, having him for a roommate relieved my mind something wonderful. I kept thinking of those mysterious Hoods. All wrapped up in their green robes, they looked like spooks going to a haunting. And what, I wondered, did they do to runaways?

As an experiment, I opened the door and poked my head out into the corridor. Right away, a hovering Hood came running up to me. "Where do you think you're going?" he demanded in a buzzing voice.

"Just to the bathroom," I said.

In the boys' lavatory down the hall, misspelled insults were scrawled all over the walls. Some of the students had let out their resentments. PUKEY MISS STINGER HAS 2 DUCK FEET. POO ON HOODS. PROFESSOR DRONE IS A WORMS BELLYBUTTON.

As I strolled back along the corridor, the suspicious Hood watched me out of two sharp gleams in the dark space where its face ought to have been. In my room again, I didn't trust the rickety chair, so I stood and stared out of my window at the brick chimney, watching the dusk thicken and two or three bats come out early.

"Hey, Timmy!"

Well, I'd be darned! Verity's room was right below mine! I poked my head out of the window to find her looking up at me.

"Hi, neighbor," I whispered down to her.

"Timmy, I'm starving. How can we possibly last till breakfast? Aren't you guys hungry?"

"Not Fardels. He's stuffed full of fish and is having a bear-nap."

"Wake him up and see if he has anything fit to eat in that old leather sack of his. I'm coming up!"

"How——? You can't come up here. Remember what Mademoiselle Stinger said——the Hoods will get you!"

"They'll never know," said Verity, swinging herself out of her window and digging her fingers into a thick brown vine that clung to the brick wall. In a minute she had clambered up it. She swung herself in through my window and hit the floor.

The thump of her sneakers on the floorboards woke

the bear. He grunted, sat up, and growled, "What's going on?"

"It's only me," said Verity. "Fardels, what have you got to eat besides raw fish?"

Fardels untied his sack. "Here's a leftover sandwich. Only a few toothmarks in it. Or what about some blackberries?"

Verity and I gobbled up those good sweet berries gratefully.

"How'd you get here, kid?" the bear asked.

"Climbed."

"Hmm. Risky. Anybody see you?"

"Nah. Those cops in the green hoods must be even sleepier than you are."

No sooner were the words out of her mouth than a knock thundered at the door. Verity glanced around to see where she could hide, but in that bare room there wasn't any such place.

"See you in the morning, fellas," she whispered, and swung herself out the window again.

Just in time. The door burst open. Two tall policemen in green robes and hoods came swooping in, making a whirring sound.

"Where's the girl?" one of them demanded in a low, menacing drone, raking the room with his eyeballs. His shadowy hood didn't show the rest of his face.

"What girl?" I asked innocently.

"The one who just climbed the vine. Was she your sister?"

They had caught us. "Yes," I admitted, "but please, Mr.

Hood, don't do anything to her. You see, we're new here and we're only just learning the rules. My sister's gone back to her room. She's promised to stay there the rest of tonight."

This explanation seemed to satisfy the Hoods, for without another word they turned, glided back out, and slammed the door. I listened out of the window and heard them in the room below, threatening Verity.

Fardels snarled, "Shall I drop on down to the girls' floor, boss? I could beat up those hooded creeps—"

"Hold on," I told him, "Verity isn't in any danger. They're just giving her a talking-to."

Soon, from below, came the slam of Verity's door. I could hear my sister laughing to herself. A minute later there was a high-pitched whining noise. I peered outside to see a Hood with a portable buzz saw slicing the old brown vine away from the brick wall. I waited till the Hood had finished his work and gone away, and then I called down through the window in an undertone, "Hey, Sis—did those cops give you a hard time?"

Her head poked out of her window like a turtle's looking out of its shell. "Not for long. They said I'd better behave or else they'd kill me."

"Oh. Is that all? Too bad about the vine."

"Never mind. Maybe I can dig my fingers and toes into the cracks between the bricks. I'll come see you again sometime."

Let me tell you, my sister doesn't discourage easily. I crawled into my lumpy old bed and lay there for a long time, wide awake. From somewhere outside came another muffled boom. Professor Drone blowing up something, probably. The moonlight shone on something I hadn't noticed before—a yellow button the size of a silver dollar, fastened to the wall next to my bed. I pressed on it, but it didn't ring any bell. It didn't seem to do anything. I didn't know what it was. Another mystery. At last I fell into uneasy dreams.

In the middle of the night, there was a loud ruckus out in the corridor. A kid was shouting. Another voice buzzed, "Try to run away, will you?" The kid shouted again and there was a loud bump, like a body being flung to the floor. I jumped out of bed, cracked open the door, and peeked out into the dim corridor. Two green-robed Hoods had a boy by the legs, dragging him away.

I turned to my bodyguard and shook him as hard as I could, but the brown bear wouldn't rouse. I sure hoped he wasn't hibernating. Anxiously, I peered out into the corridor again, but by that time the Hoods and their victim had disappeared.

Troubled, I went back to bed and lay sleepless for a long while. That poor kid, whoever he was, needed help. During the rest of the night, I kept waking up again and again. Every time I did, I'd hear a faint, menacing buzz outside our door.

5

A Highly Peculiar School

"Hey, what was all that noise last night?" a chubby kid asked a skinny kid at our breakfast table.

"It was Lester," said the skinny kid. "Lester Leafmold. The Hoods dragged him away."

"What did he do?" the first kid—who mumbled when he talked—wanted to know.

"Nothing. He went for a walk was all. I heard the Hoods say, 'Why are you out of your room?' and then they started beating up on him."

"What—what do you suppose they'll do to him?" I asked.

"How should I know?" said the skinny kid. "Chop him into little bits, probably."

I couldn't believe that. If Professor Drone and Mademoiselle Stinger allowed the mysterious policemen to kill off their students, they could hardly expect to stay in the education business. I determined to keep on looking for the missing Lester.

Breakfast at Sweetness and Light Academy was as peculiar as everything else. Slabs of beebread, with honey to smear it with. Beebread, Fardels told me, is a mixture of honey and pollen, that dusty stuff inside of flowers. He'd had a lot of experience robbing beehives and knew what it was. Nobody but bees eats beebread. Bees and the kids at Sweetness and Light.

The cafeteria had a boys' side and a girls' side, and Fardels and I were sitting with the other males, Fardels wearing his school shirt with the back split open. We all had on our school uniforms—yellowish brown outfits with black stripes running around them. If we had had wings, too, we'd have looked like a swarm of bees.

When you first went in, you pushed your tray past a steam table, where hardworking Ben Ivy forked you two slices of beebread, and then you took a seat. On every table sat a flickering white wax candle, a pot of honey, and a pitcher of flower juice. The meal was too sickly sweet for me. After everybody else at our table had had their fill, the brown bear picked up the honeypot and dumped what was left in it down his throat.

"Great chow," he said, smacking his chops.

"Where you from, kid? What's your name?" the thin kid quizzed me. He had hair like tangled string. He whined when he talked.

"I'm Tim, from Moonflower Mountain. Who're you?"

"They call me Nailkeg, because I'm tough as nails, see? Remember my name, kid. I'm from New Rockford—

the toughest place on Other Earth—and I'm the only one who gives orders around here."

"Oh?" I said. "I thought Professor Drone was the one that gave the orders."

The kid raised two bony fists. "Fight me," he whined.

"Come off it," I said. "What's to fight about?"

"Oh, so you're chicken, eh? Your liver's yellow. Bet you eat chicken corn, huh?"

And somebody else went "Cluck! Cluck!" like a hen, hoping to goad me into a fight.

"I know who you are," said the kid who mumbled, nicknamed Mumblehead. He always sounded as if he were talking with his mouth full. "You're the Eldest Elder's grandkid. Think you're a big shot, don't you? I bet they gave you the best room in this school."

"Horsefeathers. It's a crummy room, like everybody's."

"Yeah?" Nailkeg scoffed. "Pretty Boy, that's what your name is. All dressed up in new clothes for the first day of school. Well let me tell you, Mr. Pretty Boy, Mumblehead and me are the bosses around here. So you'd better do like we tell you, if you know what's good for you."

These two punks, you see, had this notion that they were really hard-boiled. I figured they'd better meet Fardels.

"By the way," I said, turning to the bear, who was swirling his long pink tongue around and around inside the honeypot, "this is my bodyguard."

The bear set down the pot. "That's right. And do you know what I do to people who bother Tim? You see this napkin thing?"

On our table sat a paper-napkin holder made of steel.

The brown bear made a fist around it and crunched it into a ball. Then he dropped the wreckage to the floor, where it clattered.

Mumblehead's jaw dropped about six inches and Nailkeg's eyes practically bugged out of his head. But the skinny kid put on a tough front.

"OK, bear, you think you're tough?" Nailkeg whined.

As hard as he could, he threw a punch that caught Fardels in his well-upholstered chest. But the big bear just looked at the kid as if wondering how anybody could be so stupid. Then he picked up Nailkeg by the back of his striped shirt and stood him upside down in the nearest trash barrel. The would-be gangster squawked, and when he struggled out of the barrel, everybody in the room almost died laughing. He had honey-covered paper napkins stuck all over him. You'd think he was a hedgehog crawling out of a can of marshmallows.

After that, Nailkeg and Mumblehead slunk away to a far-off table and didn't give us any more trouble—at the time. But I had an uneasy feeling. The bear and I had made a couple of bitter enemies.

I sat there deciding not to finish my breakfast. Idly, I turned over one of the beebread slabs. Underneath it was a slip of paper with some handwriting.

I glanced about. Nobody else had noticed my discovery. Holding my breath, I read:

I have news of your brother. Tonight after lights out I will come to your room. Destroy this.

News about Mustard! Shelley Snail's prediction was coming true. Who had hidden that piece of paper in the breakfast bread? The message wasn't signed, but when I looked up I met the gaze of Ben Ivy, behind the steam table.

Just then Mademoiselle Stinger jingled a bell for silence. We were all to write letters home, right now. Paper and envelopes were handed out, and the mademoiselle dictated what we were to write: "I am having a fine time. I am making new friends. I love it here at Sweetness and Light."

On the girls' side of the room, my sister stood up, quivering mad. "Well, I don't love it here," she protested loudly. "My bed has lumps in it. Sports aren't even allowed, and the food isn't fit for a dog."

All the kids in the cafeteria cheered wildly.

"Quiet!" shouted the mademoiselle. "One more word out of you, girl, and you'll regret it. Now write what I tell you—every word—and don't any of you dare add anything. I shall read your letters myself."

Our pens drudged. Our letters were collected. I wondered what our parents would make of mine and Verity's. Besides both being exactly the same, they wouldn't sound anything like us.

To start the day, we were all to report to the auditorium, where Professor Drone would welcome us. Filing out of the cafeteria, I caught up with Verity. In quick whispers, I told her about the message in the bread.

She was bursting with things to tell me in return. "Listen, Timmy, haven't you noticed? There's something creepy about this school. The whole place reminds me of bees. Look at this silly uniform! Don't I look like a bee? Anyway, just because you got a message, don't think you're so special. *I* got a message this morning, too!"

"You did?"

"Actually, it's to both of us. From Gramp. A windmill moth brought it to my window."

She passed me a wad of paper, which I uncrumpled and read. Gramp wanted us to know that Lew's cousins, the half million beetles, had scoured the entire land, but they hadn't found Mustard. This meant, Gramp figured, that the kidnappers had taken our brother far away, to some other country. We shouldn't worry, though. Lew would find him yet.

Verity didn't say anything. I could see that she was worried sick, like me. Fardels and I sat with her in the auditorium until Mademoiselle Stinger made him and me get up and go over with the other boys. Unluckily, I had to sit next to Mumblehead, who muttered, "Hanging around with the girls, eh, you yellow chicken? When you gonna start wearing a skirt?"

I was getting ready to poke him in the snoot when a potbellied character in a long black cape ambled slowly out on stage and stood there looking down on his audience. Professor Drone, the headmaster himself.

He stood there leaning on his heavy walking stick, puffing a cigar ten inches long. His black suit had white cigar ashes spilled down the front of it. Perched on his ball-shaped head was one of those square black hats with a tassel hanging down—mortarboards, they're called—

like you'd wear to your school graduation. His eyes in his waxy white face were narrow, practically shut. He would have looked like an unbaked pie with two slits cut in its crust, only he had a drooping shoestring mustache. Really a dead-looking guy, a walking corpse.

The whole crowd of students fell quiet, staring at him. At last he spoke, slowly, lazily, in a toneless voice. "Welcome, students, to Sweetness and Light Academy. I am glad to see so many of you here. You come from every corner of the Land of the Moonflower. In the past, this school taught useless matters, such as history, art, mathematics, languages, literature, and sports. I shall change all that. Only one subject deserves studying—*bees*."

At that, a ripple of surprise went through his listeners. All the students were asking one another, "Huh?" "Is he kidding?" "Bees?"

"Hush!" commanded Drone. "The bee is the noblest of all creatures. It works hard, it is efficient, it wastes no time. It produces two of the most precious things in the world: honey and wax. It shall be the model for all of you here at Sweetness and Light Academy.

"I realize that you cannot *become* bees," Drone went on, taking a drag on his cigar. "Bees are the master race, to which none of you deserves to belong. However, if you are diligent, you can improve yourselves greatly. You must work like bees, live like bees, think like bees. With the help of me and Assistant Stinger, you shall be transformed."

His remarks struck me as completely loony. Kids could never be anything like bees. They just aren't built that way.

In the middle of his talk, our headmaster fetched a yawn, and he called, "Xizzix, and you, Trixxiz—my couch!" Two Hoods rushed out on stage, trundling a long, low daybed, and Drone stretched his tubby carcass out on it. To my amazement he delivered the rest of his speech lying on his back, puffing his cigar and letting the ashes drop on him. We would learn to identify different flowers, find out which had the most juice. We'd study honey straining, candle making, beehive building. We'd learn how to dance the way bees do. Depending on how we did on our final exams. we'd be divided into workers and drones. Being a drone, Drone said, would be the greatest reward. The drones would get to laze around and never have to do much of anything. He said all this in honey-dripping tones, in a buzzing, singsong voice.

Next, our headmaster told us that he had dynamited the school library, and he reeled off a long list of books he had had incinerated. We wouldn't have to read them after all. The audience let out a cheer, but me, I was disappointed. Some were books I had heard of—*Treasure Island, Little Women, Huckleberry Finn*—and I had expected that school would give me a chance at them. But Drone declared that all that stuff was a waste of time. Instead, we'd read a book by Mademoiselle Stinger, about the chemicals in honey—not only read it, but memorize it word for word. At that, the whole student body groaned in agony. The two Hoods walked around the auditorium, looking menacing.

Professor Drone was the laziest guy I ever saw. He didn't really like to talk, or do anything. He kept heaving sighs and calling for nectar, and the Hoods kept running up with cups of the stuff, even pouring it down his throat for him.

"One thing is uppermost in the mind of a bee," said Drone. "Mindless obedience. That is why I'm sorry to tell you that one of your fellow students has disobeyed. Xizzix! Trixxiz! Bring out Lester Leafmold!"

At that command, the two green-robed Hoods strode out on stage, holding a frail-looking kid between them— the unlucky one who had taken a walk the night before in the corridor.

Lester Leafmold rolled his eyes fearfully. "Don't sting me!" he quavered.

From his seat next to me, Fardels gave a throaty growl.

"Easy," I whispered.

"This wretched boy," continued Drone, "refused to stay in his room last night. For a month, he will be kept in a dark cell all by himself, with nothing to eat but spider-webs and water. For him, no delicious beebread, no fresh honey, no lovely nectar such as you lucky students enjoy. Ah, my students—gaze on this fool in his misery. Isn't it wiser and pleasanter to obey?"

We all sat there stunned. Poor Lester just drooped where he hung between those two faceless Hoods.

"That's enough! Let that kid go!"

The brown bear was standing up, bellowing. He brushed his shaggy bulk past me out into the aisle and, on all fours, loped toward the stage. He reared up on his hind legs again and confronted Drone and the Hoods.

"Listen, Professor," he growled, "no kid deserves this kind of treatment. Tell your cops to release him, or I'll come up there and stomp on you."

Drone's slitty eyes widened. He squirmed down deeper in his couch. The two policemen were making a loud buzz. They didn't let go of Lester.

With a bound, the bear—who moved quickly for anybody so huge—was up on stage. He shook a heavy paw at the professor. One of the Hoods lowered his head and hurled himself at Fardels. But the bear's other powerful paw came sweeping up and caught the policeman under the chin, dumping him to the floor. The other Hood let go of Lester and charged, but Fardels gave him the same treatment. Both Xizzix and Trixxiz sprawled on stage, like a couple of toppled bowling pins.

When the first Hood had gone down, his head, usually concealed, had come out into plain view. It was round, with two huge bulbous eyes and three little ones in his forehead, arranged in a downward-pointing triangle. In a flash, the fallen cop whipped his hood back down around his face again, but not before he'd given away his secret.

These Hoods looked just like Mustard's kidnappers!

6

My Unexpected Haircut

"Go sit down with the other kids, Lester," said the bear. "You're all done being punished."

Lester Leafmold flashed a grin. Before he jumped down off the stage, he gave Fardels a big bear hug of his own.

The Hoods regained their feet. One of them asked, "Shall we finish him off, Professor?" But at the moment, Drone didn't want to confront the bear anymore. Still lying on his couch, he waved the Hoods offstage. "Bear," he said, with an angry glint in his slitty eyes, "I'll deal with you later."

Then, as if nothing had happened, he went back to praising bees. He droned on and on at great length until—I could hardly believe it—his own words put him to sleep. His head sagged down on his chest and he was snoring. The whole auditorium broke out laughing.

Furious, Mademoiselle Stinger strode to the stage and squeaked, "Silence! Do not disturb Professor Drone! Assembly is over. Report to your classrooms this minute!"

While Verity and I were going into our first class, I said, "Sis, could you see the Hood that lost his hood?"

"Of course not, stupid. What did he look like?"

"He's a giant bee! They all are! They're the same bees that kidnapped Mustard."

Verity grew excited. "Then we have to send word to Gramp right away. And we've got to get out of here!"

"Not so fast," I whispered. "Let's talk with Ben Ivy first. What's his news about Mustard?"

From her desk facing the class, Mademoiselle Stinger called out, "Stop whispering, you two! Take your seats!" Fardels came lumbering in and sat down in the rear row too.

"Hang in, Sis," I told her. "Pretend you like it here."

The class was a lecture on—what else?—bees. Our teacher's voice went neither up nor down; it was a steady buzz with squeaks in it. Soon I was bored out of my mind. I stared out through the nearest window. On the front lawn in the sun, green-robed Hoods were going around doing something to the flowers, smelling them—or collecting nectar, most likely.

At lunch, when he forked my honey-on-beebread sandwich onto my tray, the hardworking Ben Ivy looked at me intently, as if to say, "Don't forget—I'll see you tonight."

When you and your tray reached the end of the chow line, you had to pass by Mademoiselle Stinger, who made sure you'd been given no more than your share. Verity said to her, "Beebread again! Always beebread! Can't we ever have a carrot, say, or a potato chip?" But with a sniff of contempt, the mademoiselle just waved her on, as you'd wave away a bothersome bug.

"Hey, this Drone is some headmaster," chuckled Fardels, removing half of his honey sandwich with one bite. "He's the sleepiest guy I ever saw."

"You're no slouch at sleeping yourself," I told him. "But, wow, you did a great job of rescuing Lester Leafmold. I could have stood up and cheered."

"Well why didn't you?" said the bear.

"I was afraid of the Hoods. They're giant bees, you know."

The bear looked surprised. Apparently he hadn't seen the fallen Hood reveal its face. "No fooling. What if I beat 'em all up?"

From the far end of our table, Nailkeg whined, "I know what you guys are talking about. You're bad-mouthing this school. I'm going to squeal on you."

Fardels gave a growl. "You do, you little punk, and I'll throw you back in the trash."

That shut Nailkeg up. But the kid was brewing trouble, I could tell.

For all but one of our classes, Mademoiselle Stinger was our teacher. She squeaked on and on about bee history and the different kinds of clover—bee-ish stuff like that. One of her lectures, though, was almost interesting. It was about how a beehive looked inside. She showed us diagrams of where the workers and drones lived, where the queen bee's eggs were hatched. I couldn't help fixing it in my memory.

Professor Drone taught only one class, called communicative dancing, and it was hilarious. We were supposed to learn those funny little dances that bees do when they want to tell other bees the whereabouts of a juicy flower bed. Now, bees dance in midair, wagging their wings, but not being bees ourselves, we had to dance on the floor as best we were able. Buzzing in bee fashion, wearing our striped uniforms, we rock-and-rolled around, waving our arms and shaking our legs like a bunch of crazies.

But the biggest treat was to watch Professor Drone trying to dance. Our headmaster went into a spin, and succeeded in getting all tangled up in his cape and tripping and sitting down on the floor on his big fat bohunkus. He just sat there, gasping for breath, his potbelly wobbling. One kid let out a snicker, at which Drone clapped his hands and brought four Hoods charging into the room. The snickering stopped right away. "This exercise has wearied me," said Drone with a yawn. "Class dismissed!"

After our evening meal, the usual beebread and honey, we were packed off to our rooms with copies of the mademoiselle's book to memorize by morning. Flipping the pages, which were full of mathematical equations, I was in despair. I'd never learn all that stuff. To make matters worse, two Hoods came to the door and told Fardels that Drone wanted to see him. At that, the bear put on his ripped school shirt and went off with them, leaving me alone. I called this bad news down to my sister in the room below.

"Don't worry, Timmy," she called back. "Fardels can beat up six Hoods any day, and Professor Drone too."

But I felt uneasy. I could hardly wait for lights-out, when Ben Ivy would come by. Oh, why didn't Fardels return? What could the Hoods be doing to him?

All of a sudden my door swung open wide, and in barged a couple of uninvited guests. Nailkeg and Mumblehead. Nailkeg was holding a rope.

"Just thought we'd pay you a little visit," said Nailkeg, grinning nastily.

"Yuh, that's right," mumbled Mumblehead. "We got lonesome."

The mumbly kid grabbed me around the shoulders while Nailkeg forced my hands behind my back. In a moment they had tied my wrists with the rope and wrapped its other end around my ankles. Mumblehead jerked it tight and I fell to the floor, helpless as a calf at a rodeo.

Nailkeg slipped off the wristwatch that Dr. Weedblossom had given me and stuck it in his pocket. Now I wouldn't know what time it was on Mars.

"Ain't Pretty Boy got a nice room, Mumbles? What say we straighten it up for him?"

And he overturned my dresser. All the drawers slid out, spilling my possessions onto the floor. While Nailkeg was doing this, Mumblehead was jumping up and down on my weak bed as hard as he could. Ping!—Ping!—Plop! The rickety springs busted through. A couple of kicks reduced my feeble old chair to kindling wood.

"What's this?" Nailkeg whined, grabbing something out of my spilled stuff. It was this really neat bird's nest I'd been saving. He threw it down, stepped on it, and crumpled it to dust.

"Huh huh huh," Mumblehead chuckled, grabbing a pair of underpants by the fly with both hands and ripping it in two.

I was fit to be tied. In fact, I *was* tied. That rope had me all curled up, with my head and feet tugged together. Nailkeg picked up my tube of toothpaste, squeezed it all over my pillow, and smooshed the soapy stuff all around. Then he ripped the shirt pocket off my school shirt, right there and then, while I was wearing it. Next he discovered my secret diary and read parts of it aloud, jeering and sneering. He grabbed up the beeswax candle that lit the room, and burned holes through all my memories.

But the worst thing they did was to my photo collection. I really treasured it, because it had pictures of Mother and Dr. Weedblossom and Gran and Gramp and all our friends. It even included the snapshots Mustard had taken during our last picnic.

"Well if it isn't a picture gallery," said Nailkeg. "Ain't that nice. Let's make *more* pictures for the kid, shall we?"

And methodically, he began tearing all the pictures into four parts and throwing the pieces out of the window.

That really set me off. "Listen, you rat, you rip up one more picture and I'll have Fardels Bear pulverize you!"

"Ha! That's a laugh! We seen the Hoods come and take your bear away. He ain't going to bother us."

Now his grimy hand was holding my favorite picture of Mustard.

I saw red. Tied up though I was, I struggled to my feet. Head down, I threw myself across the room and butted him right in the pit of his stomach. The stringy-haired kid went "Oof!" and dropped the picture. But Mumblehead stuck out a foot and tripped me, and I sprawled to the floor again.

"What'll we do to him now, chief?" Mumblehead asked, giving me a boot in the ribs where I lay.

How much more damage could they do? All my things had been trashed and my room was a total mess. But leave it to Nailkeg to think of more mischief.

"Pretty Boy needs a haircut," he said.

He produced a little scissors, knelt down on the floor where I lay, and started to saw—those scissors were dull—at a hunk of my frontmost hair. The hunk came loose and he tossed it out the window. He sniggered, and began chopping away at my topmost part.

"Look out!" Mumblehead yelled.

Just then—to my great joy—someone in a bright red nonschool shirt and slacks landed with a thud on Nailkeg's back. Two arms gripped his neck in a wrestler's hold—a hammerlock. None too soon!

NOTE BY VERITY: *Well, I'd have come to help Timmy sooner, but I was trying to read Mademoiselle Stinger's boring book through a magnifying glass. I happened to glance out the window. Big flakes of something white were drifting by. At first, I thought it was snowing out.* Then I heard Nailkeg's voice in the room overhead, so I went out the window and dug my fingers and toes into the spaces between the bricks and climbed.

Mumblehead was still free. He grabbed Verity and tried to drag her off his partner, but she wouldn't let go.

Still caught in Verity's hammerlock, Nailkeg gasped, "Mumbles, take her glasses off! She'll be blind as a bat!"

Nailkeg, you see, was the brains of the outfit. Mumblehead, the stooge, only did what he was told. He snatched off Verity's thick glasses and flung them into a corner. That didn't prevent Verity from tightening her grip on Nailkeg, but now she couldn't see Mumblehead at all. The mean stooge sidled around in back of her and grabbed her by the hair. Trussed up on the floor, I couldn't help. Oh, it was a bad scene.

Just then there came an angry growl, and a thousand pounds of brown bear charged into the room.

"Let him up, Verity," said the bear. "Save some of him for me."

Then Fardels stuck his head out into the corridor and bellowed to the lurking Hoods, "Hey, Xizzix and Trixxiz! Nailkeg and Mumblehead are in the wrong room!" And he grabbed the two punks, one at a time, by the scruffs of their necks and the seats of their pants and flung them out of the room and slammed the door. Verity worked on my knots, and soon I was free.

I retrieved my sister's glasses for her. "Good work, Fardels!" she cried. "How come the Hoods let you go?"

"All Drone did was threaten me. He was hopping mad, of course, because I'd made him let that kid Lester go, and one of the Hoods offered to give me a taste of his stinger. But Drone said, 'No, no, the queen—' Just like that. So I figure we're under her special protection. Hey, Tim, what happened to your hair? Looks as if something was chewing on it."

"Something was. A couple of skunks with scissors. It'll grow back, I guess. But they totaled my photo collection."

I scouted around the wreckage of my room until I found Mustard's picture. It was still OK. I dusted it off and stood it on top of my upside-down dresser. The happy thought hit me that I could put my photo collection back together again. At home, I still had all the negatives.

Just then there was a loud buzzer. *Lights-out.*

Fardels flung off his torn school shirt, jumped into bed, and whoofed out our candle. The room went dark, but a full moon was shining through the window as bright as day. Verity and I sat down on the floor to wait.

At long last we heard footsteps in the corridor. A cautious knocking sounded on our door.

7

Our Furtive Friend

"Queen Meadea will stop at nothing," said Ben Ivy, "until she owns the Moonflower."

Seated on the floor of Fardels's and my suddenly chairless room, our new friend talked in a low voice, telling us everything he'd been saving up to tell. Moonlight streamed in upon his face. For the first time, I had a good look at him. I really liked what I saw. Ben had a good-humored twinkle in his eyes. I guessed that he'd been born with a sort of a little hill that he carried on his back. Because it made him bend over slightly, he had to look up at you from under his brows. But that didn't make any difference. Listening to his soft, mellow voice explaining things clearly and patiently, I figured he was one smart, nice guy. He'd read a heap of books. He knew plenty about bees and everything.

"Ben," said my sister, "aren't you taking an awful chance by coming here?"

"Not really. The Hoods are used to seeing me everywhere. I'm the handyman, the cook, and the janitor. I go all around cleaning the toilets and replacing burned-out candles."

"How long have you been doing this?" I wanted to know.

"Ever since a month ago—since the bees seized Hemlock School. You see, I used to be assistant to Professor Hemlock. When the bees told him he couldn't teach anymore, the poor old man died from a broken heart. As for me, I was demoted to a drudge."

"What a waste!" said Verity. "I wish you were our teacher, and not that boring Mademoiselle Stinger!"

"Tell us about the Hoods," I said. "They really are bees, aren't they?"

Ben nodded. "Those green robes are only a disguise. Drone doesn't want it known that it's bees who run this school. For now, he wants to hide that fact from any visitors. By the way, the Hoods aren't male, you know—they're worker bees."

Verity looked puzzled. "You mean it's *female* bees who do all the work?"

"That's so," Ben affirmed. "The only males are the drones, and they lead an easy life."

"It's not fair!" said Verity in outrage. "If I was a worker bee, I'd—I'd go on strike."

Some things didn't make sense to me. "So why did the bees want to take over this school?"

"Queen Meadea plans to come here and start a new colony. Her old hive has run out of room. And with this school for their base, the bees can take control of the Moonflower."

"Then—the queen hasn't arrived?"

"Not yet. But as soon as she decides the time is right, she'll come flying in, along with thirty or forty thousand of her bees."

"Ben, how do you know all this?"

"Oh, I've heard Drone talking with Stinger. The two of them and the Hoods—they're only scouts. Drone and Stinger came to the Land of the Moonflower and did some exploring. They figured that our school had room for a whole new hive."

Verity blew up. "That horrible Stinger! That mean Drone! They're nothing but traitors to people!"

"But loyal to their queen," said Ben with a sad grin. "After all, they're bees themselves, don't you know? The mademoiselle is a hardworking worker. The professor, though, is the laziest drone who ever snoozed."

I'd had a vague feeling that our headmaster and teacher weren't quite human. Now I knew why.

"Those two," I said, "must have messed up Hemlock School something fierce."

Ben Ivy sighed. "I wish you could have been here last springtime. Oh, this was a happy place back then. But ever since Drone arrived, he's been doing his best to destroy it—even using dynamite."

"You mean—?"

"He's been blowing up things—the playing fields, the

observatory, our handsome old brick library. He wants to leave nothing of the old school but a single building. We'll become a beehive surrounded by flowers."

Drone's fondness for dynamite explained the booming noises I'd heard the previous night. And the stack of rubble in the backyard—that must have been the library.

"You may not realize it," Ben went on, "but you and all the other students are hostages."

Here I'd been thinking that the bees' only hostage was Mustard!

"Well, aren't you?" Ben went on, seeing us look stunned. "Isn't that why the Hoods won't let any student leave this school? And why is Drone so determined to turn you all into bees? So that you'll be faithful servants of the queen when she starts her new colony."

Fardels Bear wrinkled his forehead in thought. "OK, if you know so much, tell us—why did the bees kidnap Mustard?"

"Because they wanted to capture all three of the Eldest Elder's grandchildren. Tim and Verity were coming to school anyway. But not Mustard. Him they had to come and seize."

"I get it," said Fardels. "They think that if they have all three of Elder Tibb's grandkids in their power, he'll do whatever they say."

"Gramp won't ever give in!" said Verity. "He knows that if only giant bees can drink from the Moonflower, then the other insects will starve. And the whole country will shrivel up and die."

"I wonder what your grandfather will do," said the

bear thoughtfully. "Oh, I wouldn't want to be in his shoes."

"Ben, you said you have news of Mustard," I persisted. "Do you know where they've taken him?"

"Yes—to their hive."

"And where is that?"

"I only wish I knew. Somewhere far from here, where there's no chance of rescuing your brother."

"Oh is that so?" rasped a small, familiar voice. "Well let me tell you, buster, that's a lot of horsefeathers. There isn't anyplace we couldn't rescue the kid out of, if we only knew where it was."

"Lew!" I cried gleefully. "Is it you?"

"So who did you expect?" said the detective. "Napoleon? Didn't I tell you kids I'd drop in on you? OK, so the bees took Mustard to headquarters. That's the clue I've been looking for. Now all we have to do is locate that buzzing old hive."

"How?"

"Think I'll just take me a flyby through Professor Drone's apartment. Something tells me they're keeping late hours, him and that squeaky lady. There's a light on right now in his living room. I'll just cruise in and spy on 'em. Maybe I'll get lucky and overhear something. That's one advantage to being tiny, junior. A little squirt like me can slip in under a giant's nose."

In a movie I saw once, Superman threw back his cape and flew. That's how Lew took off. He just threw back his rounded wing cases and stretched out his inner wings and took to the air like a superhero going to battle.

An hour went by—two hours—while Ben and Verity and Fardels and I sat in the dark, not talking much, listening to the muffled boom of things being dynamited outside. The moon, which had hung high in the sky, was beginning to sink when at last it showed a hard, armored body zipping into the room again. The ladybug detective landed on my knee and folded his flying wings and brought his spotted wing cases neatly down over them.

"OK," he said, "those two birds blabbed, all right. They sure are a couple of stinkers. That Drone is one mean dude, and as for the mademoiselle, she's got a face that could curdle a cuckoo clock and a personality to go with it."

"Well? What did you find out?" Verity wanted to know.

"Drone has sent another letter to Moonflower Mountain, and again, he's signed the queen's name to it. They've given Eldest Elder Tibb seventy-two hours to stop all the bugs from drinking out of the Moonflower. The letter didn't tell him you kids are prisoners. It only mentioned Mustard. I guess they're saving you to surprise the old man with, in case he keeps holding out on them."

I gave a groan. "Then if we're going to rescue Mustard, we have less than three days!"

"What's worse," went on the detective, "that hive is a long way from here. It's right where Dr. Weedblossom guessed it was. On April Fool Isle."

"How far away is that?" Verity asked.

"About thirty degrees north latitude and fifty-eight degrees west longitude," said Ben Ivy matter-of-factly. "You could fly there in a few hours."

"We have maps in the little blue blimp," I put in excitedly. "Let's go!"

"Hold on, junior," said Lew. "When I was cruising over the roof of this dump just now, I noticed something. The bees have let all the air out of your blimp bag. That thing is as empty as a politician's promise. It isn't going anyplace, and neither are you. You're staying right here, where at least you're more or less safe. Me and the bear will go rescue Mustard."

"We're coming too!" my sister cried.

"Kid, are you stark raving nuts? I can't let you take any risks like that. This April Fool Isle sounds like the scariest place in the world. Remember what the doc told us. Not just bees, but everything else there grows to giant size."

"Well, you said so yourself, Lew," I pointed out. "A little bug can slip in under a giant's nose."

"Now forget it, the two of you!" snarled the detective. "If I let you go to April Fool Isle, I'd be washed up. Finished. I'd have to turn in my badge. Your grandfather would fire me so fast—"

"Listen, Lew," I argued, "Mustard needs to be rescued right now. Think! How long would it take Fardels to hike all the way back to Moonflower Mountain? And how long would it take you to organize a whole new rescue party? By the time you finally rescued him, Mustard would have white whiskers. Think, Lew. You've got a rescue team right here, ready to go—the four of us!"

"That's right," my sister chimed in. "All we have to do is pump up the blimp."

The detective's face was expressionless. After a long time, he said slowly, because he never liked to admit he was wrong, "Yeah, maybe you have a point there, sister. With that seventy-two-hour deadline, there's no time to waste, that's for sure."

"Now you're talking, Lew!" crowed Verity. "Timmy can drive the blimp to the island real fast, can't you, Timmy?"

"You bet," I said, trying to sound surer than I felt.

Ben Ivy had an idea. "Suppose I can find a way to make the blimp airworthy. When would you want to depart?"

"The day before yesterday," said Lew sarcastically. "Well, as quick as we can leave. Bees do a lot of dozing in the nighttime, so we'll go before dawn, while they're still groggy. OK, kids, you win. When your granddad hears about this, I'll get my head handed to me, but OK, OK, we need to act fast. Pack your toothbrushes. If Ben Ivy can help get the blimp in the air, we'll scram out of this old honeycomb on the double."

"That's if," Ben Ivy mused, "the Hoods will let you."

"So what if they can sting?" growled the bear. "Who cares? I've been stung lots of times. Every time I've knocked over a hive."

"You forget," said Ben, "that those were ordinary bees. But a *giant* bee has a stinger like a pneumatic drill."

A sudden chill hit me, like a block of ice slithering down my spine. Verity, though, was bubbling with excitement. "Let's go! Let's go! I can't wait to get out of here!"

"*That you shall not do,*" spoke up a hollow, droning voice. It had come from the round yellow button on the wall—that mysterious button I'd wondered about.

"*I have heard everything,*" went on the toneless voice of Professor Drone. "*You children need a lesson in obedience. Attention, all Hoods! Destroy the little blue airship at once! Dynamite it! Blow its cabin to splinters! Blast its balloon to a thousand thousand shreds!*"

8

"Blow Up the Little Blue Blimp!"

So, all this while, Drone had been listening to us through that yellow button! I could have lain down and died.

"*Blow up the little blue blimp!*" Drone ordered the Hoods. "*Arrest those Tibb kids and their bear, and that snooping ladybug!*"

"Quick! Follow me!" shouted Ben Ivy.

And he barged out of the room, with the rest of us at his heels. At a bend in the corridor he shoved open a swinging panel in the wall. LAUNDRY, it said on it.

"Jump in!" Ben urged. "Down the chute, everybody!"

An ominous droning sound was coming closer. The Hoods were on their way.

I didn't need a second invitation. While Ben held open the door to the chute—a slide that you threw bedsheets down so that they'd fall to the basement and get washed— I hopped right in. The chute was steep. I shot down it like a bullet. In another second my feet thudded into a wash basket piled with sheets. Two seconds later, my sister landed with another thud, kicking me in the back.

"Ooof!" I said, all my wind knocked out. "Couldn't you have waited till I got out of the way?"

NOTE BY VERITY: *Well, after all, we were trying to escape from a bunch of giant bees. Really, Timmy should have moved faster.*

My sister and I scrambled down onto a flagstone floor. More wash baskets stood all around, overflowing. The bedsheets gave off a musty smell. I figured that nobody had done the wash lately.

Thud! Ben Ivy landed beside us, with a chuckle like a kid hitting the dirt at the bottom of a playground slide. "Come on, Fardels!" he called up the shaft. "Hurry!"

But we had a new problem. The brown bear was stuck in the chute. He had dived in headfirst after us, but his big, shaggy body had wedged fast.

"Keep going, you guys," he rumbled. "Don't wait for me. Looks like I'm not going anyplace."

Thinking to grab Fardels from below and tug on him, Ben Ivy tried to walk up the chute, but it was too steep and slippery. The ex-assistant headmaster just toppled back down into the wash basket.

Lew Ladybug was sitting on my shirt collar. "Holy smoke," he said. "The Hoods will be there any second. They'll nab the bear for sure."

"Can't we do anything, Lew?" I wanted to know.

"Beats me, junior. There's no way anybody can yank that fat blob of bear meat down here."

Fardels was growling and grunting and wriggling, trying to work himself loose. But he couldn't budge.

On the upper floor we had quit, the droning was now so loud it hurt your ears. A whole pack of Hoods must have arrived. I pictured them standing up there, inspecting the bear's hindquarters.

"*Owww-oo-oo-oo-oo!*" Fardels let out a wolflike howl. Then came the *whoosh* of his huge body falling, and a loud crackling as he landed on the wash basket, smashing its wicker sides.

"Fardels!" cried my sister. "Are you all right?"

The bear stood up, rubbing his bottom. "Yeah, I think so. One of the Hoods must have helped me down. He started to prod me with his stinger."

Lew was all business. "Listen, Ivy, what's the best way out of here? Now that these overgrown bees know where we are, they'll be swarming down here any minute."

Ben thought fast. He broke into a smile. "There's an old tunnel the bees don't know about. Let's see—"

Swatting aside a mountain of bedsheets, he uncovered a wooden door in the wall. He tugged on its rusty handle. With a creaking of hinges that hadn't turned lately, the door swung wide, revealing a brick passageway stuffed full of spiderwebs.

"Through here!" Ben urged. "This is a tunnel the gardeners used to use. It leads to the toolshed outside."

Fardels, who had been rummaging a packing case, was cramming something waxy into his mouth. "I'll just bring along a few loaves of this beebread," he said. "It might come in handy."

A steady buzz was fast approaching the basement. We barged into the tunnel. A spiderweb swatted me in the face. I almost choked, but I spat it out. Underfoot, the bricks were slimy and cold, but slipping and sliding, fingering the walls, I groped my way along. Verity, who didn't find darkness any problem because she couldn't see much light anyway, was ahead of me. Fardels, on all fours, brought up the rear—but where was Ben?

Our friend had lingered behind us in the basement. "Go on, all of you," he called after us. "The Hoods aren't chasing me. I want to talk to them—I have an idea!"

He shut the tunnel door after us, and I could hear him dragging wash baskets across it, hiding it. Now what, I wondered, could he have in mind?

In minutes—we stopped only to soothe the feelings of a spider who complained that we had busted its web, and didn't we have any respect for craftsmanship?—we arrived at a flight of wooden steps leading upward. We took the steps two at a time and emerged in an old, disused shack cluttered with rusty rakes and hoes. Through the only window, whose glass had fallen away, we peered outside.

On the moonlit lawn in front of the academy, a squad of green-robed Hoods was marching back and forth, chanting, *"Blow up the little blue blimp! Blow up the little blue blimp!"* Our airship, its balloon squashed flat and its cabin lying on its side, sprawled useless on the grass in front of the school.

"Those honey chasers must be fetching the dynamite," Lew said dryly.

The thought of the blimp blown to pieces—my little blue blimp—filled me with desperation.

"Lew, we can't let them! We've got to stop them, Lew!"

"Yeah," agreed the detective. "But how?"

"Hold on," Fardels growled, "something funny is happening out there. Am I seeing things or isn't the blimp getting bigger?"

Before my astonished eyes, a couple of Hoods were working a big silver pump, making a handle go up and down rapidly. With a steady *puff—puff—puff,* air was rushing into the blimp's collapsed bag, filling out its wrinkles, making it plump again.

"Blow up the little blue blimp!" chanted the Hoods.

I could have cried for joy. "Sis! The Hoods are inflating the blimp for us!"

"Don't be silly, Timmy! Why would they do that?"

"Because they don't know any better," said Ben Ivy with a chuckle, stepping out of the underground stairway and into the shed. "You see, bees only follow orders—they can't interpret them."

He was laughing so hard now, he had to hold his sides. When he could talk, he explained. "I told the Hoods I'd give them what they needed to blow up the little blue blimp. So I gave them—not dynamite, but a pump!"

Tense as our situation was, the rest of us busted out laughing too.

"Oh, Ben, I could kiss you!" said my sister. And she gave him a healthy smacker on the cheek.

The bent-over guy looked embarrassed, as if he wasn't

used to anybody showing him any affection. But somehow, I thought he didn't really mind.

"You'll have to move fast," he said, "before Drone and the mademoiselle arrive. I'll stay here—I have one more little thing to do."

"OK, into the blimp!" barked Lew.

We flung open the toolshed door. Through the dazzling moonlight, Verity and Fardels and I sprinted over the grass. The brown bear, loping with powerful strides, was the first to reach the blimp. A green-robed Hood taller than the rest, in charge of the pumping party, looked up and yelled "Stop!" and held up an arm—or bee's leg, as I guess it was, really. Fardels swung a paw at her and knocked her sprawling.

Two more figures had appeared on the lawn. One wore a ruffled blouse, and the other the cape of a professor.

"What's the meaning of this?" Professor Drone roared, glaring at the seventeen or so Hoods. "I told you to *blow up the blimp!*"

"We did, master," said a Hood meekly. "Do we not always obey?"

Drone was so mad he was hopping up and down. "No! *No! NO!* You idiots! I didn't mean to pump it full of air! I meant *dynamite* it!"

Stinger squeaked, *"Arrest those children and that bear."*

At that, all seventeen Hoods swooped forward to grab us. And then—

Boo-oo-oo-oo-mmmm!

A blast trembled the ground under our feet. For one bad moment, I thought the blimp had burst, but no, the little airship was bobbing merrily on its mooring line. The explosion had come from behind us—from the tool-shed we had just left. All of a sudden the shed was a jumble of broken boards. A cloud of purple smoke billowed out of it and rolled over the lawn.

And then Ben Ivy was at my side, grinning, holding a burned match. "I dynamited the shed to distract them. The Hoods can't see you—the smoke has dimmed the moon. Quick, here's your chance! Get on board!"

And he lent Verity two cupped hands to step into, and she did, and he boosted her through the blimp's open doorway. Fardels picked me up and tossed me inside after her. Then he grabbed the anchor—the sack of cement—and threw it into the blimp, climbed aboard himself, and latched the door.

The Hoods were milling in confusion. Drone and Stinger were bawling commands that nobody heard. Set free, the blimp had begun to rise. Now we were floating a few feet up in the air.

"So long, Ben!" my sister shouted through a porthole. "You've been wonderful! But won't Drone do something terrible to you?"

"Don't worry about me!" Ben shouted. "Have a good flight!"

Through the pilot's window I could see Drone dimly through the smoke. He had run after us, waving his walking stick. He lifted a leg and aimed a kick at our cabin door. But already we were too high up for him. He lost his balance and fell over backward and flopped to the ground, completely losing his dignity.

Lew, perched on the control panel, twittered at me, "Come on, junior, start the motor! Get us out of here while the getting's good!"

I pushed in the starter button. Behind the cabin, the blimp's propeller sprang to life with a reassuring *whizzzz.*

Ben Ivy stood below, waving good-bye, grinning from ear to ear. Drone, too, was looking up and waving at us. Only *he* was waving his fists.

The little airship darted up, up, rising over the smoke and clouds, searching for the moon. Sweetness and Light Academy shrank away beneath us. The night was clear now, and perfectly bright.

Were we out of danger? No way. A fearsome buzzing noise sliced through the nearby air. The Hoods had shed their robes and revealed themselves as bees. Their wings unfurled, they had lit out after us, flying faster than the little blue blimp could go.

Lew, staring out of the pilot's window, rasped, "Here come five of 'em. All in a swarm. *Look out!*"

I stared. In front of the blimp, the swarm was hovering. They had turned their rear ends toward us, stingers extended. They were going to bore a hole through our balloon and make us crash.

"OK, bear," said Lew Ladybug coolly, "ready with the antiaircraft fire?"

"Ready," Fardels growled.

To my amazement, the brown bear was holding a small bundle—three sticks of dynamite tied together—and a matchbox, which he offered to my sister. "Hey, Verity, will you light this fuse for me?"

"Sure," said my sister, "but why don't you light it yourself?"

"I—I hate to admit this. I'm scared of fire."

"Why, you big baby!" my sister said. She scratched a match and the fuse began hissing like an angry snake.

"Thanks," said Fardels, and he kicked open the cabin door. Like a baseball pitcher, he cranked back his right arm and hurled the bundle straight at the nearest Hood.

Whammm-mm-mm!

The blimp rocked like a ship in a storm. I had to cling hard to the pilot's seat.

The dynamite hadn't hit the Hood dead center, but it had gone off close enough to knock her out. Wings stiffly extended, she went into a slow downward spiral and was swallowed by a cloud bank below.

"Good eye, bear," said Lew. "But—uh-oh. Here comes the Chief Hood herself. She looks mean. Any more bombs?"

"Nope," said the bear, "that's all Ben gave me."

"Rats," said Lew. "What a time to run out."

In a cold sweat, I kept staring through the pilot's window. Sure enough, the Chief Hood was roaring straight toward us, flying backwards, her stinger thrust out like a lance.

The cabin door was still flapping on its hinges, open wide. Now Fardels was picking up something long and heavy and lumpy and flinging it out through the doorway into space. The Chief Hood wasn't a yard away when the missile beaned her with a loud, dull *conk*. Her head sagged on her neck. She went into a tailspin, dropping fast, and next thing I knew, she had disappeared.

Lew gave a whistle of admiration. "Neat shot, bear! What in the heck did you hit her with?"

Fardels turned to my sister. "Sorry, Verity. I owe you a new bagful of lifting weights."

"That's all right," said my sister. "Just be sure you get the kind that go up to fifty pounds."

Without their leader, the other Hoods hung in the air uncertainly. While I continued to worry, they circled the blimp once or twice. I watched them soar past the pilot's window, so close I could see the hair on their underbellies. But with no one to give them orders, they didn't know what to do. Finally, they turned around and buzzed away. We'd seen the last of the giant honeybees—for a while.

Everybody cheered. The blimp's nose broke into a sky full of the new day's sun, just coming up now, blazing with gold.

9

The Stolen Shark

"We made it!" bellowed Fardels.

The bear clapped me on the back with a heavy paw, making me hit the control stick and send the blimp into a sudden dive, which I quickly had to pull us out of.

"Wheee-e-ee!" went Verity.

"Don't bug the pilot, bear," said Lew harshly. "There's a five-hundred-mile ride ahead of us. Maybe if we're lucky we'll get there before dark."

Now that we were cruising smoothly—there was an automatic pilot I could switch on to keep the blimp on a steady course even when nobody was at the controls— the first thing I did was to peel off my Sweetness and Light uniform. I had a ratty old T-shirt and pants kicking around the cabin, so I pulled them on and flung my hated old bee-striped clothes out of a porthole and let them go flapping away.

We glided over woods and pastures and vineyards, which looked unbelievably green. We barged through a rain cloud and out the other side, and the rain washed our windows and made them sparkle like diamonds. We munched some of the sweet, waxy beebread that Fardels had brought. After breakfast the bear, with a mighty yawn, sprawled on the cabin deck, and my sister pillowed her head on his chest, and soon they were both asleep. I was too excited to want to sleep, myself. At the controls of the little airship, I felt gladder than I'd felt in days.

Soon we were crossing an ocean where whitecaps nodded and pitched. Dolphins somersaulted by, like families of waterwheels. We were flying over the Gulf Stream of Other Earth, a river that flowed through the surrounding sea, its water bright blue and clear and filled with tumbling seaweed the color of gold.

I broke out a chart and spread it out on deck, and Lew flew up and down it till he located the dot that was April Fool Isle. To keep us headed in the right direction, the detective stationed himself on that dot, like a little red pushpin on the chart.

"Tell me something, Lew," I asked, "have you ever been scared?"

From his spot on the map, the ladybug detective glared up at me. "Sure, kid. Who hasn't been? Why?"

"I'm such a coward, that's all. Maybe not so bad as I used to be, but I still get scared just from thinking. About this April Fool Isle we're going to. About the bees. And I wonder—how can I ever be like you, and be brave?"

"Listen, sweetheart, nobody's brave all the time. You

bet your bottom dollar I get scared. Why, when I was a grub, I was always quaking in my skin, afraid some robin would get me. Being scared—that's no disgrace. You go ahead anyhow and do what you have to do. Take Fardels. He's afraid of fire, but when those Hoods were chasing us, he was throwing dynamite."

"Lew, even if we find Queen Meadea's hive, how do we rescue Mustard? We don't dare walk into that hive. Won't the bees see us right away and—and sting us to death?"

"Just drive your blimp, junior," said the detective coolly. "That's a problem, all right, but I'm working on it."

Verity woke up and wanted a turn in the pilot's seat. All she had to do was keep us flying in a straight line, so I took a break and let her pilot for a while. Once, though, she almost slammed into a seagull, and the bird shrieked, "Watch out where you're going, will you? You almost clipped my tailfeathers!"

NOTE BY VERITY: *Timmy WOULD have to mention that. But the seagull wasn't hurt, not a bit. And I'll bet he kept away from blimps after that. Maybe he learned a good lesson.*

Fardels piloted for a while, then I took over again. It was late afternoon and the bear was looking out of a porthole when he gave a shout:

"Land ho! It's April Fool Isle!"

Sure enough, in the deep blue ocean below us, a tropical island gleamed. Cliffs of rock, high and purplish blue, rose from a ribbon of shore. There were rich green hills and fields of every-colored flowers. I threw the control stick forward and sent the blimp into a downward glide. With a soft bump, we came down on a powdery white sand beach at the foot of some high purple cliffs.

Fardels threw open the cabin door and tossed out the anchor and we piled out. You'll excuse me for bragging, but I had brought the blimp down on a beach so narrow that a blanket spread out on it would have got soggy.

NOTE BY VERITY: *OK, Timmy, quit blowing your own horn.*

Tied to its anchor, the little airship bobbed in the wind, lightly slapping the beach like a busy punching bag. I stared up. Rocky cliffs climbed straight into the sky for seventeen miles.

NOTE BY VERITY: *Always exaggerating. Those cliffs couldn't have been more than TWO miles high.*

Two miles, then. Laughing and shouting, my sister and I galloped up and down the beach, she hanging on to the tail of my T-shirt. It was great to feel the spray in our faces, to hear the steady boom and shush, boom and shush of the waves.

Then Fardels gave a yell. "Tim, look out!"

A tremendous round blob as big as a bathtub came hurtling out of the sky, missing me by inches. Like a bomb going off, it hit a pile of rocks on the beach and smashed, shattering pieces of thick gray shell in all directions. A big black clam with one waving foot lay on the rocks, exposed, and half a second later, a seagull swooped down and gobbled it. The gull had dropped the clam on the rocks to bust it open. You aren't going to believe me, but that gull was the size of an elephant.

While I was still recovering from that narrow escape, I had another scare. With a whine like a buzz saw, a flying shape drove straight down at us. For a moment, I thought the bees had arrived, but no, it was a mosquito. Not one of your everyday swattable kind. This mosquito was as big as a helicopter.

"Duck, Sis!" I cried, yanking Verity down flat on the sand. We huddled there while the giant insect came drilling toward us. Its wings revolved with a deafening whir.

But the brown bear didn't flinch. He just stood there on his hind legs waiting for the giant to come close. When it was almost on top of him he reached up and grabbed it by its long pointed nose and gave a twist.

"Yow!" wailed the mosquito. Its wings stopped rotating, and its long skinny legs kicked and flailed. The brown bear reeled it in like a boy bringing a kite down out of the sky. Keeping a paw clamped around the monster's nose, he laid it out flat and planted a shaggy foot on top of its belly.

"What's the big idea," he demanded, "attacking strangers like that?"

"Well, I was thirsty," said the mosquito in a stifled voice.

"Let it up," said Lew. "I want to ask it something."

Looking reluctant, Fardels allowed the mosquito onto its feet, but he kept a tight grip on its nose.

"All right, Slim," Lew said to the mosquito, "we're going to let you go. But before we do, tell us—what's the quickest way to the big bees' hive?"

"Won't talk," said the mosquito. "Bees would kill me. Find out for yourself."

"Shall I twist its beak some more, boss?" the brown bear wanted to know.

"Never mind," said the detective. "That wouldn't do any good. OK, Slim, you have to promise not to give us any more trouble. And don't tell the bees about us, either. Is that a deal?"

"All right. I promise." Wrinkling its injured stinger and muttering under its breath, the giant insect collected its legs and wings and whined away.

On a rock by the water's edge sat a remarkable bird—a fish hawk with brown wings, a white head, and angry eyes. This hawk wasn't normal in size. I've been on buses it would have made two of. Something struggled in its beak—a flash of fins. The giant bird had caught a whole live shark.

NOTE BY VERITY: *Why wasn't the shark a giant, like the osprey and all the other birds, animals, and plants on April Fool Isle? Because it lived in the ocean, I guess, where everything's natural.*

"Ha, it's another one of the locals," said Lew. "Bear, go ask it if it has seen the beehive lately, will you?"

Fardels looked dubious. "Does that thing eat meat?"

"Nah," assured the detective, "it's an osprey—a fish eater. What's the matter, you scared of a bird?"

The brown bear gulped, straightened his shoulders, and marched up to the enormous hawk. "Hello. How are they biting?"

"Catch your own food, you lazy bum," muttered the osprey, talking with its mouth full.

Just then a terrific wind beat down on us. It knocked

the bear and Verity and me flat. It flung Lew down on his back on the sand, where, legs waving, he had to rock back and forth to right himself. The osprey was swept off its perch. The hungry bird gave a squawk as the captured shark flew out of its beak, did a flip in the air, and disappeared.

That's right. *Disappeared.*

"It's that eagle again!" the osprey shrilled. "The dirty supper-snatcher! Darn her, I never can see her coming."

Lew gave a long, low whistle. "How do you like that? That must have been the giant invisible eagle Doc Weedblossom was telling us about."

The osprey was having a fit. "It's not fair! I *work* for a living, and the eagle doesn't! She's nothing but a thief!" With a few other bitter remarks, the huge hawk spiraled away. Somehow I didn't feel too sorry for it.

We lay low, hiding under the moored blimp, expecting the eagle to return, but she didn't. She must have carried the stolen shark up to her nest.

"Don't look now," said Lew, "but here's more company."

A colossal round dome of shell was crawling along the beach in our direction. It moved slowly and ponderously on legs that looked thicker than tree trunks. It must have been the size of a house.

Verity could see its dark mass. "Timmy, what is it?"

"A tortoise, I think."

This giant moved with dignity. He took a long time to reach us, for he made a lot of stops along the way. When he finally arrived, he sat there inspecting us with great half-closed eyes, his head wobbling in the air.

"Please, sir," I asked him, "can you tell us the way to Queen Meadea's hive?"

The tortoise opened and closed his mouth twice, and then said, "Sorry, sonny, but I can't help you. I don't pay any notice to bees. I keep my eyes to the ground, minding my own business. If other folks did the same, this would be a better world."

I must have looked disappointed, because then he added, "Ask in the village, why don't you? The people there would know."

"A village? Are the people giants?"

"Nah, they're like you—little fellers. Their kind haven't lived here long enough to grow to decent size. Why, I can recollect when their great-great-granddads first came to this island. Must have been a hundred and fifty years ago. Back then, I was just a little waddler, myself, but let me tell you, sonny, I sure did like to eat. Ant eggs, in particular. Kind of salty, they were, nice and warm and real good tastin'. I tell you, boy, there's nothing better than to shove your beak right smack-dab into one o' them colonies. And did those mama ants ever get riled! Why, I recall the time—"

"OK, Pop," Lew cut in, "shut off the memories, will you? Just tell us where this village is. We haven't got all night."

"Oh, in a hurry, are you? I declare, it seems like everybody's always in a hurry nowadays. Well, I'll tell you, you just follow this road till you come to a fork, and then you turn right. The village is another three, maybe four, miles. Crazy as loons, them people that live there. You'll see what I mean, likely enough."

Thanking him, we left him to shuffle on, dragging his massive shell, carving a deep groove in the sand as he passed.

10

The Village of Practical Jokes

Up in the air in the little blue blimp again, we kept seeing more wonders. I sort of hate to tell you about them. You'll think I'm making it all up.

NOTE BY VERITY: *You can believe my brother, for a change. I couldn't see all those things myself, but I was there.*

OK, there was this snail that would have made a million Shelleys.

NOTE BY VERITY: *Forty-five thousand Shelleys, maybe.*

It must have been over twenty feet high, with horns like pole vault poles, and it moved along on a leathery foot the size of a whale. There was a mouse lots bigger than Fardels, with ten-foot whiskers, and an earthworm half a block long. What's more, all the plants on the island were giants too. Bananas grew four feet long, and I noticed a skyscraper-tall sunflower. Every place you looked you saw something that couldn't possibly have been. Only it was.

"There's the village," said Lew. Through the pilot's window I could see a cluster of roofs poking out of the trees. I eased forward on the joystick, and we started dropping. Red roofs, tilting crazily, rose to meet us. I dodged them and set us down in the middle of the village square. These people, I figured, weren't giants. All the houses were normal in size.

Once, the square must have been covered with grass. But now it was nothing but a field of mud, with patches of weeds as tall as pine trees. We clambered down, moored the blimp to a giant dandelion, and glanced about. I expected the villagers to come running out for a look at our airship, but there wasn't a soul on the street. Where were the people? Was this a ghost town? I stood listening to the silence, feeling beaten down by the sun of late afternoon. Everything wobbled and shimmered in the heat, as though it wasn't exactly for real.

TOWN HALL, said a sign, ALWAYS OPEN. We rattled the door, but the place was locked up tight. Spiderwebs covered its windows. The steeple was missing its bell.

Hoping to meet somebody, we walked the village streets, peering into the windows of closed shops. Every one of them had joke goods on display. Rubber chickens. Plastic snakes. Black ink spills made of tin. Drinking glasses cut with flowers that would drip, trick bandages that would shoot right off your finger into somebody's face. Fake black eyes, celluloid vampire teeth, imitation rubber throw-up, phony bullet holes ready to stick to panes of glass.

Fardels was walking along next to me. Suddenly, the

bottom half of him dropped out of sight. I heard him roar, and looked down to find him stuck up to his waist in an open manhole. I gave him a hand and, grunting and straining, he managed to climb back out.

"What happened?" I asked.

"Don't know," said the bear. "All I did was step on a manhole cover."

I took a look at the manhole that had trapped him. All around its edges hung shreds of torn paper, as if the hole had been a circus hoop that some trained dog had jumped through. What remained of the paper was black, printed with a waffle pattern. Before the bear had fallen through it, it would have looked like any old normal manhole cover.

"That was a booby trap," snarled Lew. "Stick together, everybody. Keep your peepers working."

A fresh surprise lay on the sidewalk ahead of us. A beautiful big red apple. It shimmered before my eyes like a mirage. Hungrily, I stooped to pick it up, and as I did, it went zipping out of my reach and shot into a doorway. It had a string attached.

As I was standing there feeling gypped, a character with rolling eyes poked his head out of the doorway and grinned at me.

"April fool, stranger!" he cried. "That apple was rubber anyway. Here, have a cigar!"

"I don't smoke," I said.

"Lucky for you you don't. That cigar would have—hee hee!—blown up in your face. Well then, how about some nice yummy chewing gum?" And he held out a fake-looking pack with one stick sticking out.

I'd had my finger snapped by that kind of mousetrap before. "No thanks. Look, mister, can you tell us where to find the hive of the giant bees?"

"Certainly. Why, look—in the sky! There goes the queen bee now!"

I followed his pointing finger. I couldn't see anything.

"April fool!" shouted the goofy guy again, nutty with glee at having hoodwinked me.

"This place," said Lew, "is as wacky as a canary doing push-ups. Can't anybody around here give us a straight answer?"

The villagers had been hiding from us. Now they came bubbling out of every doorway in the square and surrounded us, grinning like crazy. They looked terribly skinny and frail. Their clothes were tattered rags.

"Welcome, strangers!" said a woman in a tattered dress. "Wouldn't you like some nice cold lemonade?" A pitcher in her hand made a clinking sound like rattling ice.

Would we ever! Our throats, from all the heat, were as dry as sandpaper. So the woman poured Fardels and my sister and me each a glassful, and we eagerly gulped. Then we sputtered and spat. The drink wasn't lemonade—it was warm seawater.

The woman gave a hysterical laugh and dumped the pitcher upside down. What had rattled inside it hadn't been ice cubes at all, but a bunch of seashells.

Fardels gave a deep-down growl. He said to Lew, "Want me to teach these jokers some manners, boss?"

"Wait," said the detective. "I don't like their crummy

tricks either, but these clowns are harmless—so far. We need to get directions to the hive."

And now, all around us, the streets of the village were springing to life. Paving stones in the street turned out to be rolled-up banana peels, and people were stepping on them and skidding and making crash landings. A lady opened her sun umbrella and a shower of white mice fell out. "Wait till I catch that scamp of a nephew!" she shrilled. Firemen in red uniforms rushed around with buckets, answering false alarms—but their buckets were solid wood with painted water. A mother came by pushing a baby carriage, but the passenger wasn't a baby. It was an alligator—or some giant alligator's baby, seven feet long, a mean-looking thing that kept chomping its jaws. I hated to guess what would happen to anybody who peered into *that* buggy to say kitchy-coo.

I leaned against the side of a brick building, only to have the whole ten-story structure topple over backward away from me. It had been built with soft soap between its bricks instead of cement.

"Everybody in this village is loony," said my sister, shaking her head. "Can't we get out of here?"

Just then a bellow from Fardels spun me around. The brown bear was waving a paw at the village square.

"Hey, Tim, take a look at what those jokers have done to your blimp!"

I gaped. Bobbing at the end of its mooring line, the little blue blimp wasn't blue anymore. Now its bulging balloon shone bright green with white stripes, like a giant watermelon. The villagers had painted it.

"They've ruined it!" I wailed. "How can we ride in a watermelon?"

NOTE BY VERITY: *Lew was really mad at those jokers. I could tell he was, because he'd started to smell just awful. You see, when ladybugs are annoyed, a strong-smelling liquid starts oozing out of their elbows. Honest, I'm not making this up. It's true.*

"Where are the cops?" rasped Lew. "Who's in charge of this screwball country anyway?"

"Oh, you mean our Prince Jester!" exclaimed the woman with the pitcher. "We'll take you to him! Right this way!" And she cackled as if something bad was going to happen to us.

"To the palace!" bawled the guy with the rubber apple, and the crowd took up the chant, "To the palace with them!"

Eagerly, they started pushing and dragging us. Lew, who'd been keeping out of the sun under my collar, snarled, "Who are they shoving?"

And yet, surrounded by that crowd, what could we do? Not a thing but be helplessly swept along.

11

Princess or Baby-sitter?

Half pushed, half carried, we passed through twisting streets littered with booby traps of banana peels. At last we came to—what was it, a spook house from some broken-down amusement park? Out of windows thick with knotted-string spiderwebs, all sorts of fake menaces leered. Bedsheet ghosts, dummy skeletons, plaster vampires— none of them looked real enough to frighten a flea. The doorbell, stuck with a pin, kept ringing constantly.

In front of this palace on a jittery throne sat the Prince Jester himself. He was a thin, bald man in a worn-out clown suit with a red rubber carnation pinned to it. His greasepainted face was divided in two: the left half paste-white and happy, the right half dark blue and sad.

As the mob shoved us up to the foot of his throne, the Prince Jester rose on jittery legs. He looked at us, giggled, and said in a nervous, scatterbrained way:

"Strangers, approach! What brings you? What? A complaint, you have a complaint? Well, out with it! What is it? Speak!"

Lew Ladybug skimmed down, landed on an arm of the throne, and glared. "*I* want to complain, Your Majesty or whatever you are. Everybody's playing jokes on us. This bear fell through a paper manhole. Some wise guys painted this boy's blimp like a watermelon. So what are you doing to do about it?"

Half of the prince's face looked serious—the half with the downturned mouth. "Do? What shall I do? I'll fix everything! Painters—back to your pots! This time, paint the blimp to look like—like a pickle!"

This command made a hit with the crowd. They hooted at us, hollered, and jeered. Then they whipped out water pistols and squirted us with something wet that smelled like rotten eggs.

Verity couldn't take any more. "Don't you dare pickle that blimp, you clown!" she yelled. "Timmy, give me one of those water pistols!"

I snatched one out of a villager's hand and gave it to her, curious to see what she'd do. Squinting through her heavy glasses, she fired the water pistol straight at the Prince Jester. By luck, she hit him smack in the eye. The one on his happy side.

At that, I expected a police car to come screeching up and police officers to arrest us and throw us in jail. But no, the crowd howled with laughter, and the prince had a fine time capering around mopping his dripping eye, pretending to be furious.

"Revenge! I'll take revenge!" he cried. He probed his pants pocket, found the squeeze bulb that worked his red rubber carnation, and squirted Verity.

Lew had been growing steadily madder. "Listen, buster," he snarled up at the prince, "I don't know what your game is, but I've seen funnier ones in nursery school. I guess you'd better tell your jokers to fix this kid's blimp back the way it was—quick, before a Kodiak brown bear kicks the tar out of you."

The Prince Jester cocked his laughing eye at Lew and cried, "Look out, little bug! Here comes a seagull to gobble you!"

Lew leaped, but there wasn't any seagull, of course.

Quaking with merriment, the prince was about to sit back down when Verity sounded an alarm. "Look out, Prince Jester!" she shouted. "Your throne is on fire!"

She was right. While the prince had been standing, some joker had touched a lighted match to his chair cushion. My sister couldn't see worth a darn, but she could smell smoke and hear the crackle of flames.

"Ha," scoffed the prince, "do you take me for a baby? Such an old joke—did you think I'd fall for it?"

Chuckling, he plunked himself down onto the blazing throne. Three seconds later, his eyeballs almost shot out of his head. With a yowl, he sprang into the air, madly swatting the seat of his pants. In back of him, the old wooden throne he'd vacated went up like a torch.

Then something surprising happened.

Nobody laughed. The crowd just stood there staring at my sister, their mouths open wide.

At last one citizen found his voice. "That girl—she wasn't joking! She told the truth!"

"Truth?" echoed the crowd, as though they hadn't heard the word lately. All fell to muttering with their neighbors. The mutter swelled into a roar.

"She tells the truth!" people were shouting, as if they'd never heard anything so strange. Next thing we knew, they were swarming around Verity, all gabbing at once, pressing her with questions they wanted straight answers to:

"What year is it?"

"Are we at peace or at war?"

"Have you seen my mother? She's been missing for ages—"

"Silence, all of you!" commanded the Prince Jester. "I want to question this young woman myself. Tell me, young woman, why did you warn me about that fire?"

"Because," said my sister, "I didn't want you to burn yourself."

"Incredible," murmured the prince. He beckoned to a man with a long white beard. "Ezra, my friend, what do you make of this?"

Ezra hobbled forward. He spoke haltingly, carefully choosing his words. "Your Royal Witticism, this girl has reminded us of something. We've forgotten about the truth. We've been too busy fooling one another. That's why we're in misery. Nobody farms and nobody fishes, nobody has enough to eat. If it wasn't for the banana trees we'd all have starved long ago. Our clothes are in rags, but there's no replacing them. Why, look at my shoe—I have only one, and you can see my toes through it. But we don't make shoes. We make false faces, exploding wallets, chewing gum with red pepper in it."

The prince looked sad now, on both sides of his face. "But aren't they good fun? All these wonderful joke goods we've made?"

"I grant you," said Ezra, "they *used* to be fun years ago, back when all this joking started. We wanted to laugh all the time. But something went wrong. The jokes are on *us*. And now they just aren't funny anymore."

"He speaks the truth too!" cried someone else in the crowd.

Ever so slowly, the Prince Jester lifted his arm. With the sleeve of his clown suit, he wiped the greasepaint from his face. His whole mouth was fixed in a straight line. "From this moment on," he declared, "I am no longer the Prince Jester. I am the Prince again." Then he looked at Verity pleadingly. "How can we tell the truth again? The way you do?"

"Why, it's easy," said my sister. "You only have to want to, I guess."

Out of the crowd a voice hollered, "Hey, Princey, duck! Here comes a chocolate cream pie in your face!"

But there wasn't any pie, and right away, the heckler was surrounded and hushed. Soon all the people were talking together earnestly. They were going to plant crops, shear sheep, write poems, build fishing boats again. Some of them produced axes and began to trash their joke-goods stores. The air turned loud with crashes and splinterings.

"Away with false faces!" the Prince Jester cried. "No more fake inkblots, phony finger-bandages, rubber cockroaches! I ban them! From now on, we'll have nothing but the truth."

"Mister Prince," my sister objected, "what's wrong with *some* of those things? Couldn't you let people play jokes once in a while?"

After consulting with old Ezra, the prince agreed. From that day on, people would be allowed to play jokes on April Fool's Day—or on any other day they really wanted to.

Mysteriously, the stolen bell had been restored to the town hall steeple, and now it gave out a cheerful clang. Dancing began in the streets, to the music of dusted-off instruments that hadn't been played in years.

That night there was a feast in the village square. Verity and the rest of us sat next to the Prince Jester at a long table piled high with giant bananas. All the while we dined, the prince kept looking at my sister admiringly.

"Stay here with me," he begged. "When you grow up you shall be my princess. Together, we'll rule this land."

Verity reddened. "Oh, no," she said quickly. "I thank you, Your Highness, but really, I couldn't stay."

"And why not? Am I not handsome?"

"I—I don't even know what you look like. I can't see much of anything at all."

"Then touch me," urged the prince. Hesitantly, Verity placed a hand on his wrinkled cheek and ran it down his face as far as his knobby Adam's apple.

"There," said the prince, when she'd finished her inspection, "am I not a noble figure of a man?"

Uh-oh, I said to myself, he's asking for it. My sister would tell him the truth—what a wreck he was. I hadn't ever known her to fib. It was pathetic to see the prince waiting for her answer, with hope in his watery eyes.

Verity's reply was slow in coming. At last she said, "You're a prince, so I guess you must be noble. But please understand—Timmy and I have to find our brother Mustard and go back to the Land of the Moonflower where we belong. Thank you for asking me to grow up and be your princess. But I can't stay here just now."

"Not just now?" said the prince. "Does that mean you might come back—someday?"

Verity appeared to be struggling to hold back hurtful words. "I—I'll think about it."

Her reply dumbfounded me. No girl in her right mind, I figured, would dream of marrying that poor old bag of bones. Yet my sister had spared his feelings. This wasn't like Terrible Verity.

NOTE BY VERITY: *That was what the other kids used to call me. But I've learned something. There wasn't any reason to tell the prince EVERYTHING I was thinking. That would only have made him feel bad. I mean, it's good to tell the truth. But who says you always have to blurt out ALL of it?*

"Hurrah!" shouted the prince, leaping to his feet. I thought he was going to dance on the banquet table. "You didn't say no to me!"

The villagers sang songs and told stories. They told of the invisible giant eagle that lived on a high ledge: "the eagle as wide as the world." I figured that, since the story-tellers hadn't ever seen the bird, they had made it even bigger than it was. They would have kept us up all night entertaining us, but we were tired, so they fashioned beds for us out of their leftover whoopee cushions—those things that squawk when you sit on them—and we slept outdoors on the warm ground.

In the morning, after a breakfast of sliced bananas—the prince assured us that by the next time we came they'd have cereal to go under them—our royal host gave us directions to the hive.

"But I warn you," he said gravely, "without Queen Meadea's say-so, no one enters her domain. Don't even try, I beg you. Her bees are fierce. They'd sting you to death on sight."

"Thanks, Your Majesty," said Lew, "we've met some of those bees already. Don't worry, we'll watch out. But if we don't come out alive, it's been nice knowing you."

As our parting gift to the prince and the April Fool Islanders, Shelley, who had been dozing in Verity's back pocket, woke up and uttered this poem:

"Fresh. Happiness. Each. Fruitful. Year. Begets.—
Crops. Standing. Tall. And. Heavy. Fishing. Nets.
Farewell. Mean. Sniggers! Welcome. Hearty. Laughs.
Welcome. Whole. Princes! Farewell. Half. And. Halfs."

Even though the villagers were sad to see us go, they carried us on their shoulders to the blimp, which, I was glad to find, had been scraped clear of its watermelon paint-job and was its old blue self again. Fardels and Lew and I got aboard, but my sister was still lingering outside on the village square. The prince was taking an awfully long time saying good-bye to her.

And then—

All of a sudden there was a blast of air like a hurricane. The blimp, still moored to its anchor, jumped and pitched wildly, slinging Fardels and me to the deck with a crash. I stared out of the open doorway of the cabin. All the people on the village square had been toppled like rows of dominoes. From out of the wind came a high-pitched scream, followed by a *crunch* as a great weight landed. The prints of two gigantic bird feet appeared in the mud—feet with four crooked toes. Each print looked as big as a rowboat.

As fast as it had come, the hurricane stopped, and I guessed that the giant invisible eagle had folded her wings. Then quickly, with more crunching sounds, more prints appeared—right foot, left foot, right foot, left—hurrying straight toward Verity.

Lew, good old coolheaded Lew, sailed out to meet our visitor. When he reached the nearest footprint, he made a polite bow—a dip in the air—and said, "Morning, ma'am. I take it you're the Eagle as Wide as the World. What can we do for you?"

The eagle gave a crazy-sounding scream. "You can let me have that girl!" she shrilled. "I've had my eye on her ever since I saw her on the beach yesterday. I'm often away from home fishing, and I need a live-in baby-sitter to look after my eaglets while I'm gone. That girl will do perfectly. Oh, don't worry—I'll feed her right. She'll have plenty of fresh-caught sharks."

"Now hold on, Mrs. Eagle," said my sister, "I couldn't watch your kids. Honest, I couldn't. My eyesight is terrible."

"Fiddlesticks!" snapped the eagle, pacing around in a circle and making more footprints. "What does your eyesight matter? These babies are invisible. My stars, girl, you've got ears, haven't you? You'll know when they're crying. Come along!"

There was a *whoosh* of giant wings unfurling, and the back of Verity's shirt stretched out to a point, as if an invisible beak had grabbed hold of it. While I looked on, shocked, my sister shot up into the air and dangled high over the village, kicking furiously.

"Put me down!" she bawled.

But the eagle gave another thrash of her wings, and a fresh blast of wind threw me to the deck once more. When I could scramble to my feet again and look out, Verity was sailing off into the sky, hair streaming behind her like a banner. From the way her feet were working, you'd have thought she was running up stairs.

12

Dangling by a Thread

Tied up on the beach again, the little blue blimp swayed on its mooring line, nodding and bobbing in the wind. My feet sinking into the powdery sand, I squinted up through blazing sunlight. I was scanning the cliffs, trying to spot the eagle's nest. Those cliffs were so steep that, looking up at them, I had to lean back so far that I nearly fell over. Seagulls squatted in notches all over their face, like hundreds of white statues fixed to a wall.

"If only we had a telescope," I said wistfully.

"One telescope coming up," chirped Lew. Perched on the tip of my index finger, he crossed the transparent tips of his wings, and said, "OK, junior, take a good look."

I'd almost forgotten. That was one of Lew's talents. He could make himself into either a telescope or a microscope, depending on which way he crossed his wings. So I stared through his wingtips at the crest of the cliffs, and it leaped up close. The villagers had told us that the eagle lived on a ledge on the face of the cliffs, away up high. I squinted till I found it. It wasn't hard to spot—a long, flat, jutting shelf of rock with a huge old gnarly tree on it. Under the tree was a tangled heap of branches—no doubt the eagle's nest, built where the tree would shelter it from wind, sun, and rain. While I kept on peering through Lew's wings, a tiny figure all in red appeared, pacing back and forth.

"There she is!" I yelled. "It's Verity."

"Good work, junior," said Lew, flipping himself shut. "Now all we have to do is get her down from there."

After the eagle had grabbed Verity, the rest of us had held a council of war. Now we had *two* people to rescue, not just Mustard. Lew decided that Verity was the one who needed rescuing the fastest. Where she'd be would be pretty dangerous for anyone with poor eyesight—on a ledge two miles high up in the air.

The prince had offered to send some of his villagers along with us, but Lew had figured we'd do better to sneak up on the eagle by ourselves. Still, the prince had wanted to help rescue his princess, as he called her, so he insisted on giving us a bunch of old joke goods, like an exploding cigar and some powder that made people sneeze. I didn't see how those things would be much good against a giant invisible eagle, but anyhow, we took them and thanked him, and I stuffed them into my pockets.

Now Lew was pacing my shirt collar, deep in thought. "Didn't the eagle say she makes lots of fishing trips?"

"Yes, but if we can't see her, how will we know when she's gone?"

"Hmmm. Think I'll take me a trip up to her nest. Maybe I won't be able to see her, but I can listen for her. As soon as she's gone, I'll give you a signal. I'll have Verity throw something off the ledge. Then you guys come by in the blimp. I'll meet you and we'll pick up Verity."

The scheme *sounded* easy. A gust of wind arrived, and the detective opened his wings and stepped out on it. The wind lifted him straight up the face of the cliff like an elevator. His spotted back dwindled out of sight.

Fardels and I waited. After what seemed like hours, a bundle of bones came rattling down the face of the cliff and smashed at our feet. It was the skeleton of a fish, probably the osprey's stolen shark.

"That's the signal!" I cried, and right away Fardels and I piled into the blimp. Fardels hauled in the anchor and the blimp rose, and in minutes we were hovering just over the crest of the cliffs. A hundred yards below us, the ledge jutted out, holding a nest of flung-together branches the size of a baseball diamond. Over the nest, shading it from the sun, leaned the gnarly tree. Powerful winds had blasted it, twisting it around and around as it grew. I scrunched my eyes and made out the little red figure of Verity, sitting on the ledge, looking dejected. I couldn't see any chicks in the nest, but somehow I knew they were there.

Red-and-white wings were dancing in front of the pilot's window. Fardels unlatched a porthole and let Lew in.

"Now's our chance," said the detective, talking fast. "The mother eagle just took off. Tim, how close to the ledge can you bring this bag of gas? Somebody has to help Verity on board."

"I'll go get her," said the bear, flinging open the cabin door.

I took the blimp lower, lower, till it hung in front of the ledge. That ledge was a broad shelf of purple rock sticking out from the face of the cliffs. I inched the blimp close to it, and Fardels got ready to jump.

Then—*whoooowsshh!* A gust of wind caught the blimp and swept it higher. With a sickening *boom!* the side of our balloon slammed the cliffs. Boards groaned, and, on our cliffward side, zigzag cracks shot down the cabin wall. Everything that wasn't tied down, including the bear, flew across the cabin and smacked into the opposite wall and crashed to the deck.

"Quick, kid, take us higher!" barked Lew. I threw the engine into reverse and backed the blimp away from that rocky wall and let us float upward. There, above the brow of the cliffs, the air was still. Damaged though it was, the blimp hung safe and motionless.

"Rotten luck," said Lew. "The wind's too strong. For a minute there, I almost thought it was the eagle coming back. We can't rescue Verity *that* way."

"What'll we do?" I asked anxiously.

"I guess we don't pull alongside the ledge. We want to hang directly *over* it."

"Then what?"

"We drop a rope. Somebody goes down on it and gets

off at the ledge. He grabs the girl. Then he ties the rope around her and we haul her up and bring her aboard."

"And what happens to this somebody? The guy who goes down the rope? Do we leave him down there in the eagle's nest?"

"No, you clock-head. Soon as we pick up your sister, we drop the rope again and he grabs it and we pull him back up here too."

"Lew, that's neat! Fardels can shinny down a rope, can't you, Fardels?"

The bear looked doubtful. "I don't know—I never tried."

"Not him," said Lew firmly. "Use your thinker, kid. *You* couldn't lift a half ton of bear on the end of a rope. But a bear can lift *you*."

I must have turned pale as a fresh-washed ghost. "Who, me? *Me?* You want me to shinny down a rope two miles up in the air, next to a wall of jagged rock, with that wind blasting at me? I can't do it. I only got B minus in gym."

"Listen, Tim, all you'll have to do is dangle. Fardels will do the rest. In a jiffy you'll be standing down there on that ledge, as safe as a fresh-laid egg."

Wind howled. The cabin trembled. So did I. Oh, I was scared, completely and hopelessly.

But then I remembered Verity. "Isn't there some other way to save her?"

"Nope," said Lew.

"When—when do I go?"

"Right now. While the mama eagle's still out shark

catching. Kid, I don't like this circus-acrobat stuff either. But it looks like you're in the center ring, and the spotlight's all yours."

And so I switched on the automatic pilot and stepped away from the controls. Fardels looped one end of a rope under my arms and knotted it across my chest. He yanked on it, making sure the knot would hold. It was a secondhand rope, and it looked thin and hairy in places. Then the brown bear unlatched the cabin door.

A blast of wind came roaring in like an express train. I clamped my eyes shut tight. I took a step. Another. I stepped out through the doorway into nothing but air. I plunged down, down, for a sickeningly long time, until a sharp jerk of the rope under my armpits brought me to a stop. There I swung, like a puppet on a string, while the bear slowly lowered me through space.

I descended, alongside the cliffs, in installments of a few yards at a time. I looked down at the beach two miles below. From where I hung, it looked to be one solid mass of rocks. Tiny waves were creaming their heads against it. I stared up at the rope that held me—it seemed only a thread—and at the little wooden cabin under the bobbing blimp, where the brown bear stood in its doorway, letting me go down, down, down.

Around me, the wind rose to a shriek. It made me swing back and forth like a pendulum, my feet just grazing that purplish wall of rock.

I was having a fit of the quease. I was going to throw up. It felt better if I shut my eyes. I guessed that Verity, hanging from the eagle's claws, must have felt the same way.

I opened my eyelids a crack to see the cliffs rushing at me, jagged and rough. I'd be grated! But overhead, the bear gave a tug on the rope and swung me away again. Now the ledge was only a dozen yards below me. Verity stood there, not knowing that I dangled just over her head. I tried to shout to her, but the wind took my voice and flung it away.

The blimp must be swaying and bobbing. I started to spin around and around like a marionette with its strings tangled. My head reeled. My armpits felt sore where the rope went under them. A gull the size of a jet plane went winging past, with a shriek that almost blew out my ears.

Then from overhead came the worst sound I had ever heard in my life. A terrible, shuddering *twaann-nn-nn-ggggg!*

The rope had snapped.

I was falling. Falling with dizzying speed toward the beach and the rocks below.

13

In the Eagle's Fastness

I'm Verity. I know this an awful time for me to take over this story, what with poor Timmy falling through the air like that, but my brother says I absolutely have to tell you what it was like to be carried off by a giant eagle, and the only place to tell you about it is here.

When the eagle grabbed hold of my shirt, I started whizzing through the air so fast I could hardly breathe. All I could see was a blur. That made me glad I'm legally blind, because if I'd known how high we were flying, I'd have been scared. But when we came to the top of the cliffs, I could see the purplish blue color of that wall of rock. Pretty soon my feet touched down on a hard, flat surface—the ledge where the eagle nested. The big bird let go of me, and I fell down in a heap. There was a powerful smell of fish.

Loud squawks were coming from the middle of the

ledge. I reached out a hand and felt the nest, a pile of branches. Then came a high, shrill voice like a toddler's—only louder—"Oh boy, Mama! Breakfast! Is that a mouse?"

"No, no, Eggbert," said his mother sternly, "this is your new baby-sitter. She's going to look after you while I'm out fishing. You be nice to her!"

"I'm hungry," said Eggbert. "Hey, mouse, where's your whiskers?"

"I'll whisker you, you big brat," I said.

"Now, Eggbert," said his mother, "be polite. All right, girl, you're in charge. I have two chicks, Eggbert and Aglet. They're twins. Eggbert's the one that's trouble."

"Just like me and my twin brother," I remarked.

"See that they stay in the nest and don't fall out. Are you hungry? I'll bring you some nice fresh fish."

Before I could say no thanks, I didn't want any fish unless it was cooked, the eagle thrashed her wings and caused a hurricane that knocked me sprawling. She was gone, leaving me with these two invisible chicks.

"Want breakfast!" Aglet piped. "Don't want mouse! Want fish!"

"It's coming, baby," I told her. "Your mother will be right back—I hope."

Trying to get my bearings, I explored the ledge. I ran into the trunk of a big old twisty tree, too thick for my arms to go around. Very slowly, I walked toward the sound of the ocean, carefully using the toe of one shoe to test the rocky floor ahead of me. The ledge ended in a sharp edge with nothing but air beyond. I shivered and backed away from it. Then I made an about-face and walked as far as I could go in the opposite direction. It was a pretty long hike until I bumped into the cliff. The eagles' home was this really humungous ledge maybe two hundred yards deep and seventy-five yards wide—which gives you some idea of the big birds' size.

All the while I was exploring, the two invisible chicks kept squawking up a storm. There was a loud *bump!* and I guessed that Eggbert had fallen out of the nest. He set up such a yammer you'd think it was the end of the world.

What was I to do? I felt all around on the rocky floor until my hands met something slippery and feathery.

"I falled out!" Eggbert screamed. "Put me back inna nest!"

It isn't easy to lift an invisible eagle chick, all solid bird except for his feathers. He was a whole lot bigger than I was. But I'm a wrestler, you know, and I do a lot of real serious weight lifting. Grunting and straining, I managed to raise the chick off the floor a little, up onto his feet. He had fishy breath. He gave me a pinch with his beak, which felt like being harmlessly bitten by some giant duck.

"Can you walk?" I asked him.

"What's walk?"

"You move your feet. One foot, other foot, one foot—"

With Eggbert leaning on me—oh, wow, was he ever heavy!—I staggered toward the nest. A couple of times he fell down, but I sweet-talked him till he stood up again. I kept walking him along till we got to that tall pile of branches. He climbed part way up it, and with all my strength I boosted him. At last he toppled down next to his sister again, gurgling happily.

"Eggbert's a dope! Eggbert fell!" his sister taunted him.

Eggbert must have given her a dig with his beak, because she let out a scream and kept on screaming. Those bratty birds made such a racket I had to clamp my hands over my ears.

When they finally calmed down for a minute and I could lower my hands, I was in for a shock. My hands had disappeared! Even when I held them up close to my face, I couldn't see them. All I had was wrists that stopped in midair. But the funny thing was, I still had hands. I could feel them, I could wiggle my fingers.

As I stood there, my heart pounding, wondering what had happened to me, the explanation dawned. I'd been holding on to Eggbert. And some of his invisibility had rubbed off on me.

There was a pile of dried seaweed on the ledge, so I wiped my hands on it. As I wiped, they slowly reappeared. Part of my side was missing, where Eggbert had leaned on me. I wiped it too, and it returned.

The chicks had started to fight. Luckily, just then a fierce gust of wind arrived, telling me that the mother eagle had landed back home again.

"What's going on?" she shrieked. "What's all this fuss?"

"It's nothing," I told her. "Aglet made fun of Eggbert

because he fell out of the nest. But I got him to go back in."

"My stars! Did you indeed!" said the eagle approvingly. "How did a little girl like you ever lift a big eaglet like that?"

"I didn't lift him—I kind of walked him. Exactly how big is he?"

"Almost as big as I am. So Eggbert can walk! Good work, girl. I knew you'd be right for this job. Here, have a tuna fish. It's lovely and fresh—the osprey caught it not two minutes ago."

I said I wasn't hungry, thanks, but as you might know, Eggbert and Aglet tore through their mother's catch in no time at all. I could hear them gobbling and smacking their beaks.

"Tell me about yourself," said the eagle kindly. "You aren't from around here. What are you doing on April Fool Isle?"

I told her our story, about how Timmy and I had first blundered through the doorway to Other Earth, about the bees, how they were holding Mustard. The eagle kept still, listening, but soon Eggbert and Aglet were hollering for more fish. So the hurricane swept me off my feet again, as their hardworking mother hurtled off.

Tired out from brawling, the chicks fell asleep and soon were snoring. What a relief! I sat down on the ledge and thought about Timmy and Lew and Fardels. What could they be doing? I wondered if I'd ever get back together with my brother again. I thought about Mustard in the beehive, where he'd been a prisoner for days and days. I worried about the deadline that the bees had given

Gramp. Oh, everything looked hopeless. I didn't want to, but I started to cry.

"What's. The. Matter. Verity?" piped a shrill small voice from my back pocket.

I pulled out Shelley Snail and held it close to my eyes.

"Everything's the matter, Shelley," I said. "Tell me, what's going to happen? Will I ever see Timmy again?"

The snail withdrew into its shell. After a few minutes it peered back out again and said in its small, faraway voice:

"To. Nurse. Small. Eagles. Restless. In. Their. Nest.
May. Seem. Lost. Time. But. All. Is. For. The. Best.
Courage. Dear. Child. Deliverance. Hovers. Near.
Soon. Far. More. Than. Your. Hands. Shall. Disappear."

I didn't understand that last line, but somehow I felt better. I thanked Shelley and gave it a bit of seaweed to eat before I stuck it back into my pocket again.

And then came a happy surprise. There was a familiar little flutter in the air next to my face, like the breeze from a pea-sized electric fan.

"Ssh-h-h-h," cautioned the ladybug, "don't wake those chicks. Listen, kid, there's no time for chitchat. Your brother and the bear and the blimp are down on the beach, waiting to rescue you. Can you shove something over the ledge for a signal, to tell 'em the coast is clear?"

"Something? Like what?"

"Like that old fish skeleton. Roll it right off into space, will you? I'll be back in a little while. Don't worry, we'll get you out of here. Meanwhile, keep your nose clean."

I shoved, and the skeleton went rattling down, and Lew was gone.

Minutes passed. Next thing I knew, the hurricane landed on the ledge again. Seeing that her chicks were napping, the mother eagle let herself down gently. This time the wind didn't even sweep me off my feet. But I was alarmed. Here I had just signaled to Tim and Fardels that the coast was clear. Only now it wasn't clear at all.

That eagle was one sharp lady. She'd noticed that I wasn't too wild about raw fish, so she had brought me a branch full of giant apples. They were ripe, crisp and sweet, and I munched a whole one down to its core. The eagle perched in the twisty tree. I could tell where her voice was coming down from.

"Mrs. Eagle," I asked her, "how long are you going to keep me here?"

"Only till my babies learn to fly."

"And when will that be?"

"A week, maybe two weeks. It's hard to say—children grow at such different speeds. Eggbert ought to go first. Already, he can almost work his wings. What's the matter—don't you like it here?"

"Please, Mrs. Eagle, you're very kind to me, but I'm worried sick. Timmy is bound to get into trouble without me. And there's my other brother, Mustard, in the hive."

"I'd rescue him for you," said the eagle, "but I could never fit into Queen Meadea's hive. But cheer up, girl. You'll only be here a little while longer. Then you and your Timmy and your friends can go rescue your Mustard. If the bees don't sting you first."

"Already, we may be too late."

"You know, I really do need your help," the eagle said seriously. "That good-for-nothing husband of mine was supposed to take his turn feeding and watching the chicks. But he's been gone for weeks. I don't know if he'll ever come back to me."

I told her I was sorry. She didn't say anything more.

Then all of a sudden—*whooosh!*—she soared away, with a big blast of wind that knocked me flat. Eggbert and Aglet woke up and started bawling.

What had made their mother take off in such a hurry?

In a few seconds, I found out. With a soft bump, the eagle deposited something on the ledge. No, not something—somebody.

In the blazing sunshine, I could almost see him clearly. For a little while, he lay as if stunned. Then slowly he sat up and said, "What happened? Holy smoke—the rope broke! The blimp! Have to get back to the blimp!"

"Timmy!" I shouted. "Timmy, is it you?"

14

The Secret in the Feathers

It was me, all right. Sprawled where the eagle had dropped me on that rocky ledge. I couldn't believe my luck. I had fallen for almost two miles, yet here I was, still in one piece. That sharp-eyed eagle had dived down, caught me by the seat of my pants, and plucked me right out of the air.

"Timmy," said my sister, "what an absolutely nutty thing to do. To fall through the air like that! Why, you could have been killed."

I turned to my rescuer. "Thanks, Mrs. Eagle. You saved my life. Another two seconds, and—"

"No trouble at all," said the eagle, amusement in her voice. "But the next time you and your blimp pay me a visit, you had better use a stronger rope."

I must have grown red in the face. She had seen through our plan, and seen why it had miserably failed.

"No doubt you were trying to rescue your sister," the eagle went on. "Well I'm sorry, but I need her and I can't let her go. Make yourself at home. Now that you're here, you might as well help mind Eggbert and Aglet too."

I stared at the nest, a jumble of tree boughs and seaweed, maybe eight feet high. It took up most of the ledge, and you could have parked six blimps on that ledge and still had room left over. The nest creaked as the chicks thrashed around in it. Once I stood too close, and something pecked me.

"Watch out," said a familiar twitter next to my ear. "Those chicks are tough customers. They can make mincemeat of a shark."

Lew had lit on my shoulder. I was happy to see him, because I wanted to bawl him out.

"You and your smart ideas!" I whispered. "Letting me swing on that rotten old rope—"

"Sorry about that rope, kid. Guess you can't win 'em all. But everything turned out all right, didn't it?"

"Just barely. Thanks to the eagle."

"Play along with the old girl. Pretty soon she'll be making another food run. Then we'll beat it out of here."

"Right," I said, louder than I'd intended. "I'll be glad of that."

"What did you say?" demanded the eagle, whose hearing was as keen as her sight.

"I said, 'Right, I'll be glad to baby-sit.'"

"Well, see that you don't let Eggbert and Aglet out of the nest. They're very delicate."

"*Squawwww-kkk!*" went the delicate Eggbert. "Eggbert want a shark!"

"Now you babies be good," said his mother wearily. "I'll be back with your lunch in a little while."

And with a thrash of her wings that threw me head over heels, she soared off into the sky.

Lew didn't waste any time. "OK, Tim, can you see the blimp overhead? Wave to it, will you, and let Fardels know the coast is clear."

I searched the sky. At first I couldn't see a thing, but then the little blue blimp bobbed over the crest of the cliffs. I waved to it like mad.

"Hooray! It's coming!" I told Verity and Lew.

I stared at my sister. Something about her seemed awfully strange. Where her left knee ought to have been, there was nothing but air.

"Sis, what's happened to your knee?"

"Nothing. It's just that every time you touch one of those chicks, you pick up some kind of oil. I guess that's what makes them invisible."

Lew whistled. "So that's their secret! Lucky thing the mama eagle pinched you, kid."

"Why, what do you mean, Lewis Ladybug?" said Verity, with irritation. "If you think it's been fun, being stuck up here on a ledge—"

"Cool it, sis," said the ladybug evenly. "If you hadn't been hijacked, we'd all have walked straight into the hive. And those bees would have whipped out their stingers and run us through quicker than you could say Jack Robinson."

"Well if we don't walk into it, how do we rescue Mustard?"

Suddenly I knew what Lew was driving at. "Lew, you mean—we borrow some eagle oil!"

"You've got it, junior. Before we leave this roost, we grab us a few eagle feathers. We smear that sticky oil all over us and make ourselves invisible. Then we walk right into the hive and the bees won't know we're there. Verity, yank a few pinfeathers out of those chicks, will you?"

"Oh, Lew, I can't. They're brats, but I'm not going to *hurt* them. I'm their sitter. I'm responsible for 'em."

Lew glared. "How about it, Eggbert and Aglet? Give us some feathers, OK? Let this nice boy, Tim, pull a few out of you. You sweet chicks won't miss 'em. You'll grow lots more!"

But the chicks squawked, "No! No!" And they thrashed like a couple of invisible cement mixers.

Oh, it was rough assignment. All I had to do was yank some feathers out of two little invisible monsters, each as big as a house, while they tried to peck me to pieces. I gritted my teeth, stepped close to the nest, groped out and found an invisible feather, tried to yank on it. It was too slippery. My hand slid off. All I got for my trouble was a few sharp pecks.

If I'd been a dog, my tail would have drooped. "It won't work, Lew," I said.

"Never mind, kid. Drop down on your hands and knees and search the ledge. Maybe there's some loose feathers lying around."

I groped along the rocky shelf. Sure enough, my hand met a tremendous feather that the mother eagle must have shed. It was dripping with invisibility oil, and when I picked it up, both my arms vanished. I groped again, and found another.

The detective gave a wolfish chuckle. "Good work, junior. Hey, look, here's our ride."

Sure enough, the little blue blimp was hovering only inches from the rim of the ledge, wobbling and bouncing in the wind that never quit blowing. Fardels Bear was at the controls, his shaggy face fixed in concentration. He kicked open the cabin door and bellowed, "Come on, you guys, climb aboard! I can't keep this thing hanging here all day!"

"OK, Tim, you go first," said Lew. "Then you reach down and help Verity in too."

"Lew, I can't go!" Verity wailed. "I can't run out like this!"

The detective scowled. "Oh, you can't, huh? So who kidnapped you? The mother eagle, right? You just love being kidnapped, do you? Remember Mustard, for Pete's sake! Don't you want to rescue him?"

"Yes, but—the eagle has been good to us. She saved Tim's life. How can I leave her babies? What if they got out of the nest and fell off the ledge?"

"Listen, kid, these chicks aren't babies anymore. They're safe, believe me. You don't owe these eagles anything. Now quit yakking and get your butt into that blimp."

"Don't go, baby-sitter!" Eggbert bawled.

"Stay here! We like you!" the other chick joined in.

"*Hurry up!*" Fardels roared.

My sister glanced at the blimp, then back at the nest, then back at the blimp again. I guessed she was making one of the hardest decisions of her life.

"I'll go," she said finally. "For Mustard." She turned back to the nest once more and said softly, reassuringly, "Now your kids stay here and be good. Your mother will be right back. Maybe she'll bring you a nice big juicy shark."

I climbed up into the swaying cabin. I reached back down and hoisted Verity aboard too, while Eggbert and Aglet set up a chorus of screams. Fardels threw the joystick and we soared away from the ledge and into the sky. Behind our cabin, the blimp's motor purred like a cream-eating cat.

"OK, bear," the detective ordered, "make a beeline for Queen Meadea's place. Where the Prince Jester told us. Look for a field of blue and yellow flowers."

Verity, slumped on the cabin floor, seemed awfully quiet for a change.

"Sis?"

"What?"

"Back there in the village just before the eagle kidnapped you, the prince was taking an awful long time saying good-bye. Was he trying to get you to come back and marry him and be his princess and everything?"

"Oh shut your dumb face, Timothy Tibb, before I punch you in the teeth. Fardels, can't you make this blimp go any faster? Let's find that crummy old hive!"

15

Into the Hive

At the entrance, two big burly worker bees stood guard, working their wings, fanning fresh air into the hive. They held spears, which they'd crossed, making an X over the doorway, barring anyone who didn't belong inside. Other workers were landing, coming home, and every time one applied for admission, a guard would sniff it to make sure it was one of the family. Once we saw an intruder—a cockroach eight feet long—scoot in under the spears, no doubt hoping to rip off some honey, but it wasn't long before it reappeared. Four big workers heaved it back outside and told it, "Hit the road, bum."

The hive had been built inside a cave, its mouth surrounded by fields of giant blue asters and yellow goldenrod—flowers that the bees especially went for, I guessed. All the while we had been flying there, I'd kept glancing over my shoulder, but, to my relief, the eagle didn't follow us. I brought the blimp down under a cluster of goldenrod, where it wouldn't be seen.

"We'd better not go in," said Lew, "till we're invisible." So I broke out one of the feathers and started rubbing eagle oil on everybody. It was wonderful to see daylight shining through the brown bear's solid chest, to watch the rest of him grow dim, until, as far as you could tell, there wasn't anything there. Verity and her bright red outfit disappeared, and I, too, smeared myself all over. Soon everybody, even Lew, was out of sight. We had another feather left, which we'd brought along in case we'd need reoiling.

No sooner had Fardels taken care of the guards—he just stepped up behind them and banged their heads together—than we stole through the mouth of the cave and into the hive. Inside, we found ourselves in a tremendous huge room shaped like a globe, with six-sided cells lining its walls. It was so high you couldn't see the ceiling over your head. To tell the truth, you couldn't see much of anything, because the only light came from a few wax candles on the walls. Parts of the big room were chopped into smaller ones by walls of mud mixed with wax. The floor was bare earth, packed hard by all the legions of bees that had tromped on it.

Scores of the yellowish brown workers kept gliding past us, shuttling in both directions—some going out collecting, others arriving home, their bellies bulging with flower juice. Grains of dusty yellow pollen stuck to the body hair of these homecomers, and overflowed the sacks built into their hind legs. A steady, murmuring buzz filled the hive, like the noise of a factory.

NOTE BY VERITY: *I guess that's what the hive really was—nothing but a great big factory for producing honey, wax, beebread, and more bees.*

A tiny commotion in the air ahead of us told me that Lew was leading the way. The lack of light didn't bother Verity. She barged ahead. I followed. With the brown bear in the rear—I knew he was there because he kept growling—we made our way along. The place was so thick with jostling traffic that it was hard not to bump into any bees. Once, a large worker ran into me. I stepped aside and the worker looked around in puzzlement, unable to see what she had bumped. At last she scratched her head and hurried on. If any of the arriving bees had noticed the two guards lying unconscious at the mouth of the cave, they didn't seem to care. Nobody raised an alarm; they all went about their business. Most of the bees waddled briskly on their long skinny legs. A few of them fluttered and swooped along, now and then using their wings.

From my shoulder, the ladybug detective mused aloud, "Hmmm—wonder where these buzzers keep Mustard."

"Maybe we should listen to some bees," suggested my sister. "Maybe we'd find out something."

None of the workers hurrying past us was taking time to chat, so we decided to go into one of the inner chambers. Verity wanted to visit the nursery. I knew where it was, having learned from Mademoiselle Stinger's class the layout of a typical hive. Sure enough, we found it at the center of the cavern. BROOD NEST, said a sign over its door.

So we stepped into this tremendous tall room, its walls and ceilings covered with six-sided cells. Nurse bees wearing white caps were bustling about. There were plenty of candles, shedding a pretty good light. I was glad we were invisible, because we could poke around and see everything. I peered down into one of the vacant cells. It was like looking down a well, six feet deep, with walls of slippery white wax. A white worm lay curled at the bottom of it.

"Ugh!" I said.

"That's a grub," said Lew. "What comes out of an egg after the queen bee lays it there."

"That squirmy thing doesn't look anything like a honeybee."

"Give it time, junior. A grub may not win any beauty contests, but it knows where it's going. I was a grub once myself. Look—see that big thing in the next cell? That's an older grub, shaping up fast."

He pointed to a fat white blob with bulges where its eyes and wings were going to be. Just then its nurse arrived. To my amazement, she began spitting out something soggy.

"Yuk! What's she doing, Lew?"

"Putting a wax lid on that cell. Sealing up the grub so it can turn into a bee."

Most of the cells were already sealed. But from one of them, the lid was flying off in pieces. Something was hammering from inside, trying to get out. A hole smashed through the lid and a young bee, looking ready to fly, thrust out its head and shoulders. A nurse rushed up to it. "All right, you're born," she told it. "Grab a broom and get to work. This floor needs a good clean sweep!"

"Never saw such a lot of grubs turn into youngsters all at once," she said. "And so many of them are drones—those hard-timers!"

"Oh, don't you just hate these drones?" said the first nurse. "All they do is lie around stuffing their faces and hollering for more. As if we didn't have enough to do around here!"

"Well, we've got to put up with them. There has to be a drone, you know, for the new queen to marry."

"I wish Queen Meadea wasn't leaving us. She's a mean old queen, but she runs this colony right. And why does the new queen need all those drones to pick from—two dozen of the lazy louts?"

Outside in the main room of the hive again, Lew said to me, "Sounds as if, any day now, Queenie plans to fly out of here."

"Wasn't that what Ben Ivy told us? She's going to the school to start a whole new colony."

"Yeah, I know—it's what you call 'swarming,' kid. Bees do it when an old hive gets too jam-packed and they need more room. A lot of these bees are going to scram out of here. I bet that about two-thirds of 'em will take off with the queen."

"What will happen to this old colony?" wondered Verity. "How can it keep going without the queen?"

"You heard what those nurses said. Pretty soon a new queen will hatch out. She'll pick her a husband—one of the drones—and start laying eggs for herself. Those drones are nothing but pretty boys. All they do is hang around crooning love songs and slicking down their hair, each hoping the new queen will pick him."

"Sounds like a soft life, being a drone," said the bear.

Lew gave a nasty laugh. "Not for long it isn't. Two minutes after the wedding, the new queen's husband drops dead. The queen doesn't need him anymore."

"What about the leftovers—the drones she doesn't choose?"

"Sometimes she marries a whole bunch of 'em. In any case, they all die. The lucky ones that don't marry, the bees get rid of 'em. They starve 'em, push 'em outside, maybe even sting 'em to death."

"That's horrible," said my sister. "I wouldn't want to be a bee—unless I could be the queen, of course."

"Even then, you'd have it rough," said Lew with a leer. "You'd stay inside your hive and wouldn't see daylight for years. You'd just sit on cells, cranking out eggs. A couple of thousand eggs every day. Don't try it, kid. That grind could wear you down."

"Poor queen," said Verity. "What a boring life. No wonder she wants to travel."

"Baby," said Lew, "don't feel sorry for that tough cookie. She's bad medicine. Get a load of that sign on her door."

Sure enough, we had come to a massive door of white wax, with this threat on it in large gold lettering:

THRONE ROOM
AUTHORIZED PERSONNEL ONLY!
TRESPASSERS WILL BE STUNG TO DEATH

Standing there reading that warning, I started getting the shakes. But then I remembered that, luckily, we couldn't be seen.

"Not a peep, anybody!" Lew cautioned. "We're going in."

16

Spying on the Queen

"Your Majesty, the hour of departure is near. Even now, forty thousand workers are preparing to take to the sky. Excellent weather is promised—a perfect day to swarm."

The lazy, droning voice was familiar, and I smelled smoke from a cigar. We couldn't see the speaker or the queen, but we could hear everything from where we stood—behind a tall white beeswax throne. The room, hung with gauzy gold curtains, was as large as a basketball court.

"Yes, yes, Drone, I know," a honey-sweet, musical voice said impatiently. "Fan faster, chambermaids, it's stuffy in here. What on earth has happened to our air conditioners?"

"The two guards at the door? Somebody knocked them out. I suppose it was those cockroaches. But never fear, Your Majesty—I've sent for two replacements."

"Well, tell them to fan in more air," said the queen. "And Drone, put out that stinking cigar. Do you know, I'm a bit nervous about flying over the ocean. Why, I haven't flown anywhere in years. Look at me—I've put on weight. I'll be lucky if my wings can lift me anymore."

"Hasn't Your Majesty followed her starvation diet?"

"Oh, I've tried, but goodness knows, it's been difficult. I'm always so hungry I could scream. And what about you, Drone? You look a bit chubby yourself. Are you sure you can fly with me?"

"Well, I flew here, didn't I? But I don't plan to travel with Your Majesty. I must stay behind. Urgent business."

"Whatever do you mean?" demanded the queen in irritation. "Oh-h-h-h-h—I know what's on your mind! You want to meet the new princess, don't you? You're hoping she'll pick you as her mate, is that it? Why, you silly fop! Imagine a beautiful young princess choosing *you!*"

"Sneer if you will, Your Highness, but every drone aspires to be a prince. True, I have a few gray hairs, but I'm still devilish handsome. No young whippersnapper drone can match my love songs. May I play you a little sample on my ukelele?"

"Just you touch that awful ukelele and I'll smash it over your ears. Forget the princess. You wouldn't stand a chance with her. You're flying with me at dawn!"

Eager to catch a glimpse of the queen, I stepped boldly and invisibly out into the room. On the white wax throne sat an extra-huge bee dressed all in shiny black satin, looking very elegant. Glassy wings hung down around her like a cloak. Her slippers were woven of gold thread, and she wore gold-rimmed spectacles on her two largest eyes. She didn't wear a crown, and yet her every motion was so dainty and deliberate that you knew she must be a queen. Six chambermaids in gauzy dresses were fussing around her. One held a hand mirror, and the queen kept admiring herself in it. Other maids stood by, fanning her respectfully with their wings.

Professor Drone, our headmaster, looked glum. The queen had dashed his hopes of ever becoming a prince. Sprawled on a couch at the foot of the throne, he was holding a golden cup, and a chambermaid kept pouring him refills. Absentmindedly, he lit a new cigar, then remembered himself and crushed it out. A maid with a little dustpan whisked it away.

"Thank goodness," said the queen, "it's time for my snack. Boy, my royal jelly!"

This command wasn't directed to a bee. To my glad surprise, out came a kid with hair the color of mustard.

"*Mustard!*" I started to shout, then checked myself. Lew Ladybug, on my shoulder, let out a cheer too little to be heard.

Mustard looked pale, but otherwise none the worse for being kidnapped. He hurried forward, carrying a tray that held a golden plate with some slices of beebread and some quivering white jelly. Mustard parked the tray on a table next to the queen and retreated with an awkward bow. The queen, with great dignity, took up a golden knife and began smearing her bread with jelly. A maid with a napkin scooted forward and wiped off her feeler-tips.

Invisibly, I sidled up to Mustard and gave him a poke in the ribs. He pretty nearly jumped out of his skin. "What—?" he started to yell.

"Shhhh-h-h," I shushed. "It's me, Tim. We're here—Verity and Lew and Fardels. We've come to rescue you."

"Where—where are you?" he whispered back, looking all around for me.

"Standing right next to you. We're invisible, that's all."

"Yeah," chimed in Lew. "Right now, mum's the word, kid. Keep doing your job with the tray till we can spring you out of here."

Mustard grinned his lopsided grin from ear to ear. In all my life, I never saw anybody so glad not to see anybody.

The queen let a chambermaid pat bread crumbs from her mouth. "Drone, what is my schedule?"

"Your Majesty is to appear at Sweetness and Light Academy by noon. Mademoiselle Stinger will expect you promptly. We're holding Parents' Day, and all the students' mothers and fathers will be there."

"Why hold such a stupid affair?"

"To take all the parents prisoner."

"Whatever for?"

"We'll hold them hostage, Your Majesty. With all those people in chains, Eldest Elder Tibb will surely give in to us. But we've had one little setback. The Tibb twins have escaped."

"Escaped?" echoed the queen. "What do you mean, you blundering lout?"

"Escaped is what I mean, Your Majesty," said Drone

lamely. "They got away in a blimp. We've searched, but it's as if they have vanished into thin air."

At that remark, my invisible sister giggled. Fardels and I, too, let out guffaws.

"*What was that?*" shrilled the queen. "Who dares laugh in my presence?"

And she rose to her full height and raked the room with a furious glare. The chambermaids shrank back against the walls as if afraid for their lives, and Mustard, standing there with the snacks, cried out, "Honest, Your Majesty, it wasn't me!"

"I could have sworn I heard laughter," said the queen. "Any more impertinence and you shall all taste my wrath."

She sat down again, rearranged her gown, and fixed her adviser with a glare. "Drone, is it wise to take all these prisoners? I really don't approve of your idiotic school, nor of keeping those girls and boys locked up in it. Only one thing concerns me—starting my new colony."

Drone slumped lower on his couch. "Your Majesty calls my school idiotic? Wasn't it your idea to send me and Stinger to Moonflower Land with a party of scouts? Your orders were to find the perfect place for a new colony. And so we did."

"But do you need to make demands of the Eldest Elder? To send those awful, threatening letters—in my name?"

"The Moonflower must belong to us, I say."

"Why must it? Aren't there other flowers for our workers to drink?"

Drone gulped the dregs of his cup and held it up for more. "Ah, but the Moonflower is the juiciest blossom of them all. Doesn't Your Majesty wish to go down in history as Meadea the Great, Conqueror of Moonflower Land?"

"Huh?" said the queen with a sniff. "I don't give a hoot about history; I would like some more jelly and bread."

"Remember your waistline, Your Majesty. You'll be too heavy to fly."

"Oh, pish, tosh, and piffle. Another little snack won't hurt me. How can I fly five hundred miles on an empty stomach? Boy, more jelly! I simply can't live without another teensy bite."

Mustard scooted to the throne with another sticky helping.

"Drone," said the queen between mouthfuls, "why did I make you my adviser? You haven't the brains of a flea. Do you mean to lie there on that couch forever? Go see to the preparations for our flight."

With a groan, Drone heaved himself to his feet. "Very well, Your Majesty, I'll go. Anyhow, I'm sick of watching you make a pig of yourself."

"What did you say?"

"Er—I said I've grown rather big myself."

With a hasty bow, the professor stalked out of the throne room, shooing chambermaids aside with his walking stick. He passed right smack in front of me. It was all I could do not to stick out an invisible foot and trip him flat on his face.

"You know," whispered my sister, "I kind of like this

old queen. It's Professor Drone who's the bad egg, if you ask me."

The royal maids were fussing around the queen again, brushing crumbs from her gown and combing her silky black body hair. While she was being groomed, Lew said to Mustard, "Listen, kid, before you make another trip with that tray, let's scram. Fardels, where's that eagle feather?"

"Right here," said the bear.

"Give Mustard a rubdown. Cover him with oil like the rest of us. Mustard, stand still. This won't hurt a bit. Just don't be surprised when you start to disappear."

Mustard was turning invisible. Soon only his head floated in midair. Fardels kept rubbing him with oil from our spare feather, and in a minute he was totally out of sight.

"OK, you kids," said Lew. "When the bear holds the door open, scoot out of here."

We stole past Queen Meadea's throne. She had polished off her latest snack and was looking around for more. "Where is he?" she demanded. "That hostage with the tray?"

Just then Fardels sneezed a colossal sneeze that blew one of the chambermaids out of her slippers.

"Sakes alive!" cried the queen. "Lady Waxwing, go tell that stupid Drone to turn down the air-conditioning. There's a terrible chill in here!"

I had to stuff my fist into my mouth to keep from laughing. As we left the room, the queen was telling her maids to pack her belongings for her flight.

At the exit, we found our escape blocked by a milling mob. Forty thousand worker bees were getting ready to depart. Drone, puffing a cigar, was lazily giving orders, and the workers were brushing their hair all shiny and sleek, guzzling and filling their honey stomachs and loading their hind-leg pollen baskets. We couldn't fight our way through that crowd, so Lew said, "Let's switch to plan B. Tonight we'll bunk here in the hive. Then in the morning when everybody leaves, we'll leave too."

HONEY STORAGE, said a sign on a wall in a deserted section of the hive. Six-sided, waxy white cells were stacked up high. Fardels bashed a hole through a lid and scooped out a pawful of honey. Verity joined him in that sticky supper, but not Mustard and me—we couldn't stand any more of the stuff. Lew, who could eat pollen, found a cell half-full of that yellow dust. He jumped in and started guzzling happily.

When he came back out, making smacking sounds, he said, "You guys hide yourselves in this honeycomb and grab some sleep. I'll stand watch."

So I climbed up to one of the empty white wax cells. It was like sliding into a narrow bunk bed. I could hear Verity and Mustard doing the same, but Fardels couldn't fit himself into a cell. He stretched his invisible carcass out on the floor and soon was snoring.

"Mustard?" I called.

"Hnnnffff?" came his drowsy reply.

"What was it like—living in this hive?"

"The pits. Nothing but work, work, work. And I'm sick and tired of beebread sandwiches."

"I've been wondering—how did the bees bring you to April Fool Isle?"

"Two of them held me and flew with me the whole way. What a ride! I could see all over the world. That was fun, almost."

"Well, good night."

"Good night, Tim. Good night, Verity. Good night, Fardels. Good night, Lew. I sure am glad you're here."

"Us too," said Lew softly. "Catch some winks, kids. Unless I miss my guess, tomorrow could be the roughest day of your lives."

17

The Case of the
Vanished Chick

Zzzzzz! Zzzzzz!

Huh? What was that?

Zzzzzz! Zzzzzz! Zzzzzz!

The buzzer kept on buzzing. Sleepily, I reached up and rubbed my eyes open. And then out of a loudspeaker boomed the voice of Professor Drone:

"Attention all workers! Boy hostage has escaped! Honey-colored hair! Answers to the name of Mustard! All workers will start to search immediately! Search every corner of the hive!"

I tried to sit up, but I couldn't. I was lying on my back, cramped inside a narrow beeswax cell with walls that came up to my neck. So I just lay there, finishing the dream I'd been having, while for the next few minutes the whole hive went wild. Hundreds of searchers barged by, peering into every open cell. Luckily, when they looked into our cells, they couldn't see anything. As for

Fardels, he just flattened himself up against a wall and let the searchers rush on by.

While I was still waking up, who should come bustling along but Queen Meadea and the professor.

"To the runway, Your Majesty!" urged the headmaster. "Your army awaits. Forget that pesky boy!"

The queen sounded furious. "How could he possibly have disappeared? Drone, I hold you responsible for this. You told me there was no escape from this hive!"

"If Your Highness is going, you had better hurry."

The queen fetched a deep-down sigh. "How I hate rushing off like this. I so wanted a glimpse of my daughter the princess. And she hasn't even hatched yet."

"Ah, Your Majesty, we *could* both linger a little while longer. For the good of the race, Your Majesty, doesn't the princess deserve a look at me?"

"Why, you disgusting ukelele strummer," said the queen, "if the princess ever saw that foolish face you wear, she'd shrivel back into her cell. Anyhow, why on earth would *you* want to marry? You know, Drone, when a drone becomes a husband, he dies."

"But it's the honor, Your Majesty! The fame, the glory—"

No sooner had they gone than I wriggled out of my bunk. Some of my oil had rubbed off and my right leg had reappeared, but Fardels gave it another swat with the feather.

A river of bees was flowing out of the mouth of the cave into the sunshine of early morning. It was easy for us to step into line, too, and flow outside. The air hummed with excitement. Already, an awful lot of the forty thousand departing colonists had taken to the sky. And the twenty thousand bees who were staying behind had knocked off work, too, and were seeing the others off. Their yellowish brown bodies perched everywhere, on grass and bushes and trees, jostling for room. A thousand hung from a giant vine, like a buzzing bunch of grapes.

NOTE BY VERITY: *Oh, sure, Timmy! I suppose you counted!*

Well, there sure were plenty of them. It was all like a great big party. Some silkworms had woven a banner that said BON VOYAGE—"Have a good trip." A troop of the younger nectar collectors were showing off their dances in midair. There was even a band—well, sort of one—blowing weak and watery music out of blossoms shaped like trumpets and drumming on their hollow honey bellies.

We invisible spies crouched in the grass to watch. The blossom-trumpets sounded a wishy-washy fanfare and Queen Meadea, in a glittering gold dress and with a gold coronet around her head, waddled out of the hive, waving to the crowd and blinking through her spectacles at the sunshine, which I guess she hadn't seen since her maiden flight. Her maids skipped along in front of her, throwing buttercups and violets in her path. Second in line came Professor Drone, his chest puffed out self-importantly. The headmaster had left off his cape, the better to work his wings.

With Drone helping her, the queen managed to stagger up to a grassy ridge above the mouth of the cave. All sixty thousand bees fell silent. Then the queen cleared her throat and began, in a high, buzzing voice:

"My children—"

NOTE BY VERITY: *That was the truth. Every bee in the hive had hatched from one of her eggs.*

"Today I feel a great sadness that I leave so many of you faithful subjects behind. Thanks to your efforts, the quality of our honey is unequaled. Our wax is the wonder of the world."

"Aaaah, knock off the commercials, honey," said Lew Ladybug under his breath. "Buzz off!"

That remark made me and Mustard snicker, but my sister said irritably, "Shut up, Lew. I want to hear this!"

"And yet," the queen went on, "though the hour of parting is at hand, I feel not only sadness but fresh joy. For I fly with most of you brave workers to found a whole new hive! Farewell, dear children who remain. Swear loyalty to my daughter, your new queen—Waxidia the First!"

Obediently, all the homebodies raised a shout.

"And now, my departing army," concluded the queen, "to the sky!"

With that, she waddled down onto a runway of baked mud. Professor Drone and the other forty thousand— those who hadn't yet taken to the air—lined up behind her, single file. Then they unfurled their stubby wings and got them working so fast that their backs were nothing but blurs. With a strenuous effort the queen launched herself up off the ground. She staggered, nose-dived, looked as though she'd crash. But then with a tremendous effort she whirred her wings hard, and began to climb slowly up, up, up into the sky. All the bees on the ground cheered like crazy.

Faster than peas zipping out of a peashooter, her followers lit out after her. The sky turned dark with that huge swarm. Away high up, the swarm tapered to a point—which point must have been the queen. The cloud of them turned, and the forty thousand workers dipped their wings in farewell. Then they were gone.

"OK, folks, the show's over," said Lew. "Now we need to get back to Sweetness and Light Academy—fast!"

The blimp was right where we'd left it under the goldenrod, and in minutes we were in the air. I was in the pilot's seat again, steering a course for the Land of the Moonflower, when—

Whammm-mm-mm!

We'd struck something. Or else something had struck us. The blimp gave a lurch. From out of the air came a high, earsplitting scream.

At the moment, we were passing through a rain cloud, and the eagle, who'd made the scream, came sailing across our path. Her vast shape was covered with glittering drops of rain, which caught the morning sun and made her visible. I could see two wide wings level with the wind, two feet with curving talons like the roots of a giant redwood tree.

Then the eagle struck out with those talons—at our balloon. From overhead came a blast that seemed to shake the universe. The blimp staggered as if hit by a thunderbolt, pinning Fardels and me to our seats and tossing Verity to the deck. Then came the sickening hiss of escaping air.

"She's popped our balloon!" cried Lew.

"I—I can't control us!" I yelled, working the useless joystick frantically.

Paralyzed, I stared out through the pilot's window at the ocean revolving around and around. Helpless, we spun downward toward the pitching waves, the eagle's screams ringing in our ears.

If you've ever blown up a toy balloon, pinched it shut, and then let it go, you can imagine how the little blue blimp acted. Air whooshing out of its punctured bag, it shot around doing loop-the-loops. It kept trying to sling us up to the cabin roof, or else to the deck. Verity clung to a bench for dear life. My stomach didn't know which way to jump next.

Belted in my pilot's seat, I watched in horror as the giant eagle, outlined with raindrops, made another charge. I cringed, waiting for the blow.

But to my surprise, the blimp gave a shudder and stopped in midair. The next thing I knew we were swaying to and fro, as gently as in a swing, and the little airship was coming down, down, down in a smooth glide. The underside of the cabin bumped on sand. The eagle had caught hold of us and had set us down as carefully as though we were a carton of eggs.

When the world quit being a merry-go-round, we picked ourselves up, and Fardels shouldered open the cabin door and we staggered outside. Once again, the blimp rested on the beach at the foot of the cliffs. Its balloon, with a big rip through it, lay collapsed across the cabin roof like a limp hot-water bottle. And I knew that it could never fly again.

"Awwww," I sighed, looking sadly at the wreckage of my birthday present.

Crunch! Two huge bird-prints dented the sand. A mist from the sea had rolled in, keeping the eagle coated with moisture. Dimly, we could see her standing there before us like a jumbo jet. By now most of our oil had scraped off, so we were all about half-visible too.

Lew had his dander up. He snarled, "Look here, lady, what's the big idea? First you bore a hole through our blimp and try to kill us. Then you save our necks. Are you mixed up or something? Why didn't you just let us crash?"

"Oh, I didn't mean to hurt you," said the eagle. "But you understand, I was angry—angry with those two baby-sitters for deserting my chicks. I wanted to give you a scare, that's all!"

"Well, you certainly did," said my sister. "But baby-sitting your chicks wasn't *my* idea. You carried me off and made me do it. I had every right in the world to run away."

"True," admitted the eagle. She didn't sound so terrifying now. "You'll have to forgive me, young woman. I carried you off because I was worried about my children. And now I'm so upset, I'm nearly out of my mind. The gentleman with the spotted wings—the girl told me about you. You're a detective, is that right?"

"What's it to you, lady?" said Lew, still annoyed.

"You must help me. It's Eggbert. When I returned to my nest just now, he was gone!"

"Gone, huh?" Lew echoed. "You mean you can't see him? Isn't that the way he always is?"

"But he isn't in the nest anymore. I've searched everywhere. My little baby chick has disappeared!"

"Hmm," mused Lew. I could tell that, in spite of himself, the detective was interested.

"Oh dear," the mother eagle went on, "I just knew Eggbert would fall over the cliff someday. He's always been such an active child. Maybe the osprey stole him. Oh, what shall I do?"

Lew said, "OK, OK, ma'am, calm yourself. I'll take your case. These wandering-child jobs are a piece of cake to me. Now, if you'll kindly give me a lift up to your nest, I'll start investigating. I want to check out the scene of the crime. Tim, you come with me. I might need a helping hand."

Before I could protest, an invisible beak picked me up by the back of my shirt and hoisted me into the sky. Lew on my shoulder, we went flying up the face of those purplish rock cliffs so fast that I almost couldn't bring along my breath.

Right away, when we touched down on the eagle's ledge, Lew began his detective work. He stalked around and around the nest, looking at old shark spines, now and again squinting at things through his magnifying wing. Oh, he was thorough. After a while he flicked himself shut and said to the remaining chick, "Listen, Aglet, what do you know about all this? Where did your brother go?"

"Won't talk," the unseeable baby pouted.

"Aglet," fumed her mother, "you must help the nice gentleman."

Lew grunted, "Tim, grab ahold of Aglet for me, will you? Give me a rough idea how big she is."

Cringing, fully expecting to lose an arm, I reached out into the nest. My hand felt some feathers and my fingers disappeared. I tried to pat the chick, while she squawked and pecked at me. I walked around to the other side of the nest and patted her again. I tried to guess what she'd look like if I could see her.

I said, "Lew, she's a big, gawky bundle of fluff, maybe forty feet wide."

"Ha!" said the detective, as if these facts made sense to him. "All right, ma'am, I've seen enough here. Now will you please take us back down to the beach?"

On the shore again, Lew examined a pile of rocks. They were littered with pieces of gray shells that had once had giant clams in them. Other clams lay on the sand nearby. They had long jagged cracks in their shells, but their lips were shut tight.

The detective flew over and landed on the nearest clam, a character as big as a bathtub. As loud as he could, the detective shouted, "Hey you in there—how's about answering a few questions?"

The clamshell opened a crack, showing nothing but darkness inside. "Who wants to know?" muttered a low, cold voice.

"I'm a detective," said Lew, "looking for a missing child. Tell me, clam, how did you get that crack in you?"

"Dunno," said the clam. "Somebody picked me up and dropped me. Couldn't have been a gull. I didn't get smashed."

"Who did it to you?"

"Couldn't see."

"Why not?"

"Don't have any eyes."

Next, Lew flew back to question the eagle. "Ma'am, do you ever feed your babies clam meat?"

"Never!" said the eagle. "Nothing but good wholesome fish. Clams are seagull food. We eagles are fisherfolk."

"Clams must be tough nuts to crack. How do the gulls open 'em?"

"Why, they drop them on the rocks, smash them, and pick the meat out."

"And how high would you say they're flying when they let go of those clams?"

"Oh, as high as the cliffs, maybe. It takes a lot of altitude to crack one of these big clams."

"Clam cracking sounds like a skill, ma'am. Must take a lot of experience to do it right."

"How should I know?" asked the eagle impatiently.

Lew was twiddling his front feet, the way he does when deep in thought. "Looks like some of these clams didn't get opened all the way. I'd call this the work of a bungling amateur. By the way, Mrs. Eagle, when did you last feed Eggbert before he disappeared?"

"Why, at least twelve hours ago."

"Your Eggbert, he has a good appetite?"

"Has he ever! He eats all the time! Oh, I'm so worried. It isn't like him to go this long without a meal." A fine rain had begun to fall, and I could see the eagle's face. She looked fiercer than she really was. The lower half of her beak trembled anxiously.

"One last question, ma'am. Exactly how old is Eggbert?"

"He and Aglet hatched out eighty-one days ago. Eggbert was such a lovely baby! Would you believe it, the minute he broke out of his shell he started to talk—"

"Never mind, ma'am, you can skip the family history. This is an open-and-shut case."

"You've solved it? Then where is my Eggbert?"

"Ma'am, everything's plain as the beak on your face. Eagles stay fledglings for about twelve weeks. That means your chicks are practically grown-ups. Your daughter Aglet is almost as big as yourself. Ma'am, you can stop worrying. Your son has left the nest, that's all, and right now he's learning to fly. I'll bet you he's having the time of his life."

"What?" cried the eagle in wonderment. "My little Eggbert—grown up so soon?"

"Sure he is," said Lew. "He went for a flight, and he got hungry. Not knowing how to catch fish yet, he watched the gulls smashing clams. So he tried to do it himself, but, as you can tell from this mess he's made, he didn't get the hang of it. He didn't fly high enough, and the clams are cracked only slightly."

"Amazing!" said the eagle admiringly.

"Something tells me," Lew went on, "that pretty soon your other tot will be leaving the nest too."

"Look!" I shouted, pointing upward. "There they are now!"

Over the brow of the cliffs, soaked by the rain and made visible, two bird shapes were clumsily flying. They dipped and struggled and climbed, flapping the air awkwardly.

"It's Eggbert and Aglet!" cried the mother in relief. "Why, I never expected—I'm so proud of them! Why didn't they tell me they were leaving? I'd have packed them a lunch. Oh, I do hope they won't crash into the cliffs."

"They're doing great," said Lew. "They just need a couple of flying lessons. And if my bird book knows its stuff, you haven't seen the last of them. They'll be dropping in on you once in a while for a home-cooked meal."

"Ladybug," said the mother eagle, "you're brilliant. I'll never be able to thank you."

"Sure you will," said Lew. "You can start right now."

18

We Ride a Thunderbolt

Quickly, Lew told the eagle about the terrible surprise for our parents that the bees had planned. Told how we needed to return to the Land of the Moonflower as fast as possible.

"I know you eagles are homebodies," he said, "and not too big on travel. But you beaked a hole through our blimp bag, and now we're stuck. What do you say, lady? Will you give us a ride to school?"

The eagle let out a bloodcurdling shriek, which I figured she meant to be friendly. "As a matter of fact," she said, "I'd enjoy a flight. And it would be good experience for Eggbert and Aglet. They'll come along."

She gave another, whistling shriek that brought the two young eagles—also semivisible—swooping down from the sky. The mother eagle scolded her chicks for leaving the nest without telling her, but I could see that, just the same, she was pleased that they knew how to fly.

"Climb aboard!" she invited us.

Verity and Mustard and the brown bear clambered up on her back, slipping and sliding as they went, and scrunched themselves down in among her feathers. Lew crawled inside my shirt pocket. I offered to help the eagle find the way to Sweetness and Light Academy, so I got to sit right up front in among her neck feathers. Just above my head I could make out the outline of her sharp, pointed beak. If you turned a canoe upside down, you'd have a notion of that big beak's size and shape.

"Is everybody seated?" asked the eagle. "Then hang on tight!"

With a loud thrash, she threw wide her colossal wings. I glanced left and right, to see Eggbert and Aglet on either side of her, fanned out, silvery with rain, looking like two vast ghosts. Then the eagle raced along the powdery white sand and hurled herself into the air. Up we rose, in a spiral that slowly widened, as the wind howled in our ears. Soon we were three or four miles high, and the ocean waves looked like ripples in a puddle far below.

The eagle flew as if the whole sky belonged to her. I remembered what the April Fool Islanders had called her: the eagle as wide as the world. That was a pretty big name, but she lived up to it. For a quarter hour at a time, she would just glide, rising and falling gently, hardly stirring a feather. Then she'd give a thrash of her wings and surge ahead, laying her powerful body along the wind.

Always, she flew with the wind, never against it. Perched on her neck, I felt a breeze all the time, but we didn't ever run into any blast. We just kept cruising through the sky, passing through small drifting clouds and out again.

Eggbert and Aglet flew by their mother's side, flapping clumsily at first, but getting to be better and better fliers all the time. One of them even did a loop-the-loop. The eagle kept craning her neck, keeping an eye on them, sometimes shrieking them a word of encouragement.

"What time is it, junior?" inquired a ladybug-sized voice from my shirt pocket.

I started to glance at my wristwatch, then remembered that Nailkeg had taken it. So Lew crawled to the top of my pocket and stared at the sun. "Looks to be about ten-thirty," he said.

"We're late. It took a while to solve that case. How fast can that swarm travel?"

The detective made some quick calculations. "An ordinary little bee can fly twelve miles an hour. But giant bees go ten times that fast. Sorry to say this, junior, but by now the queen and her crowd ought to have made it to the Academy."

"Then they've beaten us there! They'll arrest Mother and Dr. Weedblossom and everybody!"

Lew didn't say anything. He just crawled deeper inside my pocket.

Before we started our trip, the eagle had been plainly visible, all covered with wet mist. But as we rose up over the clouds, the bright sun dried her feathers, and she disappeared. I could look right down through her body.

What a sight! Valleys and hills were folds in some wide green cloth that a giant had flung down carelessly. Clouds wandered by, grazing, and a river twisted and shone like a slow-moving snake made of diamonds.

I could have kept on flying like that for no end of years. Maybe I should have been worrying about the Hoods, and the queen's plot to capture all the unsuspecting parents who came to school. I should have been wondering what would happen when the bees had control of the Moonflower. But for a moment every problem in the world seemed whittled down in size. And I completely forgot to be scared.

Once we passed near a hot-air balloon, a round ball with a basket hanging under it, and I waved at a man and a woman in it. They almost fell out of their basket in surprise, to see two boys and a girl and a bear come whizzing out of the clouds—held up, as far as they knew, by nothing at all.

We flew for hours, making one stop on a mountain peak for the little eagles to rest, until the sun glittered fiercely overhead and it was noon. I remembered some landmarks, and I guided the eagle toward Sweetness and Light Academy. As we neared that unhappy place, the clouds began to look threatening, like full bags bloated with dirt taken out of a vacuum cleaner.

At last the great bird, her eyes fixed on our destination, went into a long, slow, graceful downward glide. The clouds parted, and the redbrick Academy shouldered up out of the gloom. I could see its grounds, the ruined library, the dismantled observatory. Near the front lawn was the wreckage of the gardener's shed that Ben Ivy had dynamited.

Tilting her wings, the eagle banked so that she neatly cleared the rooftop. Then she and the eaglets slowly fluttered down onto the grass about a hundred yards from the school's front door. I climbed down, with Lew in my pocket. Verity and Mustard and Fardels slid down the long slope of the eagle's back, whizzing like three fast sleds across her tail feathers.

At the eagle's suggestion, we helped ourselves to more of her oil and rubbed ourselves good, so that we were invisible all over. "Just don't get rained on," warned the great bird, "if you want to stay out of sight."

Then, while we all shouted our thanks, the three feathered hurricanes blasted off, heading out to the coast for some beakfuls of shark.

"Get your courage working, Tim," rasped Lew. "One showdown coming up!"

19

Surrounded and Revealed

Parents' Day had begun, and Sweetness and Light Academy was abuzz with kids and visitors. Invisibly, we strolled the lawn, where Hoods, their faces hidden, moved silently through the crowd, pouring drinks out of pitchers. Nectar, no doubt.

"I wonder if Mother and Dr. Weedblossom are here," said my sister. "They'll be looking for us."

"How will they see us?" said Mustard with a laugh.

Lester Leafmold, the kid Fardels had rescued, was strutting around with his mother on his arm, looking happy. Even Nailkeg and Mumblehead and their folks were there. Those two crummy kids were showing off a pile of things they had swiped, and Mumblehead was telling how the Hoods had locked them in the basement for the last two days, and Nailkeg had his penknife out, dissecting a dead mouse.

"Kid, you're a pro," said Nailkeg's old man approvingly. "All them wristwatches! Nice haul!"

"And look how good he can slash and slice," clucked his mother proudly.

While they were sitting there with oafish grins, watching the poor mouse's guts being unraveled, I took my wristwatch back and stuck it in my pocket. I would have put it on, but just then, I didn't want anybody to see a wristwatch floating around in the air.

"Those dirty birds," said Lew, waving at the parents, "are old stuff to me. Got a file on 'em so thick it would choke a horse. But I guess even a perfect country like this one needs a few crooks, or else there wouldn't be any work for us detectives."

Ben Ivy, in a waiter's white apron, was talking with four people—Mother and Dr. Weedblossom, Gran and Gramp. Gosh, how it blew my mind to see them all again! Grabbing Verity and Mustard by the hands—I had to grope around to find them—I made a beeline across the grass, bringing the other kids along.

"Mother! Dad! Gran! Gramp! Ben!" we chorused. The five of them stared in puzzlement, seeing nothing, hearing our voices coming at them from thin air.

"What's that?" said our grandmother.

"Why, it's Verity and Tim and Mustard!" cried our mother. "But I don't see them. Where can they be?"

Verity shrieked with laughter. "We're here—right next to you! Only you can't see us because we're all oily!"

"Oh, I don't like the children being invisible," said our grandmother sternly. "I want to lay eyes on them!"

"So do the giant bees, Mrs. Elder Tibb," said a flutter in the air that had to be Lew. "That's why the kids are keeping out of sight."

"What giant bees?" Gran demanded. "I don't see any of those awful things around here."

"Well, Mrs. Tibb, if you pulled the hoods off those guys in green, you'd see all the giant bees you could take."

Our grandfather looked alarmed. But it was my sister's words that had interested Dr. Weedblossom. "Oil, did you say, Verity?"

He reached out in my sister's direction. His fingertips picked up some oil and disappeared.

"Wonderful!" he exclaimed. "This oil makes light slide right around it. I've got to analyze this—I can't wait to get back to my lab! What happened, kids, did you meet the eagle of April Fool Isle?"

Quickly, we sketched our story. And we told them that the bees were holding Parents' Day to gather all the parents together and clap them in chains.

"So now," said our grandfather slowly, "they've done it. They have us in their power. I hope Queen Meadea will listen to reason."

"Don't count on it, Elder Tibb," growled Fardels, who had joined us. "The queen only listens to Professor Drone."

"What happened, Ben," asked my sister, "after you helped us escape? Didn't Mademoiselle Stinger do anything bad to you?"

Ben Ivy chuckled. "Oh, she tried her best to punish me. She locked me in the supply closet for a while, but finally she had to let me go. The bees couldn't run the school without me. They didn't know where anything was. Sandwich, anyone?"

And he offered us his tray, stacked with honey-smeared beebread cut into little triangles. Hungry though I was, I didn't feel the least bit tempted, but Verity dug right in, and so did Fardels. Mrs. Leafmold, who happened to be standing nearby, gave a strangled scream, seeing triangles fly off the tray and disappear into the middle of the air.

"We've all been so worried about you children," said Mother. "Only yesterday—those strange letters you sent! You didn't sound at all like yourselves."

"Mademoiselle Stinger made us write them," my sister explained. "She told us what to say. She wouldn't let us put in a single word of our own."

"Why, she's nothing but a dictator!" said our grandmother. "I just knew something was wrong. Why, Verity didn't say anything true and terrible!"

Gramp had an idea. "Verity, are you carrying Shelley Snail? I'd like to know what will happen. Why don't you ask it for a prophecy?"

In a moment, Shelley was sitting in the palm of my sister's invisible hand. It looked spooky to see a snail floating in the air like that. Mrs. Leafmold, who had noticed that, too, turned so pale she had to sit down on the grass and fan herself with a sandwich.

"Shelley, Gramp is worried," said my sister. "I guess we all are. Will the bees throw everybody in jail? Will they take over the Moonflower?"

After going back into its shell for what seemed forever, the little poet and prophet spoke:

"Who. Gains. Possession. Of. A. Bit. Of. Glass.
Shall. Summon. Aid. And. Peace. Shall. Come. To. Pass—
The. Weaker. Warring. Side. Shall. Bite. The. Dust.
Faces. Shall. Fall. As. All. False. Faces. Must."

"Darn it, Shelley," said Mustard, "why don't your predictions make sense?"

"Shelley's predictions *do* make sense," Verity insisted.
"Always, always, always. But sometimes you have to wait
a while."

"Huh," said Mustard. "Well, who's 'the weaker warring side'—us or the bees? Right now, I'd say the bees are
a whole lot stronger than we are, wouldn't you?"

"The. Future. Has. Spoken," said the snail, and it disappeared from view. Verity had pocketed it.

"So the future has spoken," said Gramp with a sigh.
"But it didn't tell me what I ought to do."

"Well, I know what *I'm* going to do," said Gran, her
jaw thrust out in determination. "When I meet that awful
queen bee, I'll give her a piece of my mind!"

But where *was* Queen Meadea? I scanned the lawn,
but I couldn't see a sign of her. Hadn't she and her bee
army ever arrived?

"No, they haven't shown up yet," said Ben in answer
to my question. "And Mademoiselle Stinger is having
fits."

Sure enough, Drone's assistant was wringing her

hands and squinting at the sun anxiously, as if trying to tell time by it. She had on a long purple dress that trailed on the ground. It made her look like a leaky ink bottle.

"The queen must be having a tough time getting here," chortled Lew. "Bet she can hardly pump her droopy wings. And Drone can't be too hot at flying, either. They must be making more rest stops than a bus full of beer drinkers."

One of the Hoods had noticed Ben spending a long time with our folks, so he buzzed over and told him, "Move along." Our friend ambled off, with a wink back at us. Verity and I told our folks more about Ben—what a great guy he was, how much he knew, how he had helped us make our getaway to April Fool Isle.

Just then the sky grew dark, as if an eclipse had shut off the sun. Down from the sky roared forty thousand giant worker bees with Queen Meadea in the lead, weaving back and forth in a dizzy zigzag. The new arrivals made such a deafening *Buzz-zz-zz-zz* that all the parents clapped hands to their ears. Imagine how you'd feel if forty thousand buzzing things, each six feet long, suddenly landed in the middle of your lawn party.

Some of the arriving colonists came down on the roof of the school, clearing the sky and letting daylight through. The rest settled anywhere they could. Some of them landed on the grass and bumbled around, knocking over punch bowls and thirstily lapping up the nectar meant for the guests. The queen settled wearily to the grass in the middle of the party. All the people fell back to make room for her.

Professor Drone had barely made it. Four workers had had to carry him, one holding each of his wings. When they landed they just dumped him to the ground, where he sprawled on his back, waving his legs and his walking stick.

At the arrival of the queen, Mademoiselle Stinger had come running faster than a cat at the sound of a can opener. She was all fuss-fuss. Invisibly, I snuck up close to hear.

"A thousand welcomes, Your Royal Majesty!" squeaked Stinger, with a curtsy that dusted the ground. "But where have you been? You're two hours late."

The queen's wings drooped. In back of her spectacles, her biggest eyes, usually bright, looked dull and glassy. She just lay on the grass like a lump. Two Hoods rushed over and started feeding her honey and fanning her with their trays, until by and by she appeared somewhat restored.

"Good grief, what a trip!" she gasped. "I'm all out of shape. But I can still fly farther than that weakling Drone!"

"These parents await Your Majesty's speech of welcome," said Stinger. "Before you clap them in chains, that is."

"Never mind the speech," said the queen. "I'm all out of breath. Just arrest all the people and be done with it."

While Queen Meadea lay there recovering, our fearless grandmother confronted her. Two hoods looked threatening, but Gran wasn't to be stopped. She strode right up to the queen and with flashing eyes declared,

"Your Majesty, if that's what you call yourself, enough of this foolishness. This isn't a school, it's a slave labor camp. Our children have been badly fed, taught a lot of nonsense, and treated like prisoners. Go away at once, and set them free!"

Gran's outburst brought Queen Meadea to her feet. She drew herself up to her full height, surrounded by her cape of long black wings. "Your children? What do I care about your children? I have children of my own to think about—my bees! Why did we found this outpost? Why did I make that punishing flight all the way from April Fool Isle? To build a new colony! So that in the future my children will thrive!"

"And don't forget," put in Drone, "we've come to take over the Moonflower too."

"Of course," said the queen. "We shall now imprison all parents and children, to insure our unquestioned ownership of the flower. Guards, do your work—throw all these people into cells! Slap wax lids on 'em!"

The Hoods flung back their hoods. They raised their giant five-eyed heads, peeled out of their now-useless robes, and fluttered their wings. They circled around the parents and kids at the lawn party, giving out a threatening *Buzz-zz-zz-zz,* and started closing in. It was as if they were tightening a lasso around the crowd.

Gramp strode forward, his right arm lifted. "Your Highness, stop! Free these people! I accept your demands—all of them!"

"Why, if it isn't Eldest Elder Tibb," said the queen.

"So—have you finally come to your senses? Do you agree to everything?"

"No, no, Gramp! Don't give in to her!" shouted my sister and I together.

But Gramp shook his head sadly. "Your Majesty, your demands are cruel. When the other insects can no longer drink from the Moonflower, it will mean the slow death of our land. However, you leave me no choice. These children must not suffer any more."

At my left ear, Lew Ladybug said, "OK, Tim, time to break up Parents' Day. Go ahead—play tricks." He called to the bear, "Hey, Fardels, bust things. Anything goes!"

At that, the invisible bear picked up Professor Drone and flung him halfway across the lawn. Everyone stared in amazement to see the lazy headmaster make a sensational jump like that. Drone landed *ker-splop!* on his rear end in a punch bowl full of nectar. It must have felt pretty chilly, being full of ice. Dripping wet, he climbed out of the bowl, sputtering, "Who—? What?"

"It's a trick!" squeaked the mademoiselle.

"Trick or no trick, I'm getting out of here," said Drone. "This place is haunted! Something grabbed me—some ghost!"

"Drone, stand your ground!" the queen commanded. "Guards, make your arrests!"

Now seemed the perfect moment to break out the joke goods that the Prince Jester had given us. I hadn't expected those silly items to come in handy, but now I was glad I'd brought them along. I pulled out a big brown cigar and, with my invisible hand, stuffed it into Drone's coat pocket, where he kept his own supply. Sure enough, the headmaster took it and lit it, as he always did when he was agitated. He puffed on it, looked at it suspiciously, puffed some more. I passed Mustard a package of sneezing powder and Verity a rubber spider.

Blamm-mmm-mmm!

Drone's cigar blew up in his face, making a big four-petaled smear of tobacco leaves. He stood there, muttering and sputtering.

"Help!" shrilled the queen. "I've been assassinated!"

And she broke out in a series of sneezes that practically doubled her up.

The next moment, Mademoiselle Stinger leaped about two feet into the air and gave a scream that rattled the rooftops. The rubber spider had slithered down the back of her neck.

Puzzled by their leaders' odd behavior, all the bees started milling around, making a confused buzz. I was helpless, cracked up from laughing.

Then our luck ran out. It happened—just as the eagle had warned us.

The clouds opened up. It started to rain.

Our eagle oil was slithering away, forming puddles of invisibility on the grass. Before my eyes, a bright red shirt appeared. Verity's. With every second, she and Mustard and Fardels and Lew and I were looking solider and solider.

"It's him!" bawled Nailkeg. "It's that no-good chicken runaway Timothy Tibb!"

20

The Final Jest

The rain lasted only a minute, just long enough to wash off most of our eagle oil. Piece by piece—heads and shoulders, arms and legs—we started to appear. Even where the oil still clung to us, we were wet, and with the shiny raindrops on us, you could see us plain as day. Fardels Bear emerged, a shaggy bulk with a slightly ghostly head. Once again, Lew Ladybug became a spotted red dot on my shoulder.

"Am I right?" said Nailkeg, looking cocky. "Ain't it Timothy Tibb? And that blinky sister of his, and that skunky bear!" He swung a bony fist at me—then, at a growl from Fardels, cowered away.

Slowly, Professor Drone cleared his face of the wreckage of his exploded cigar. He reached up and wrung the ashes from his shoestring mustache and sucked each end of it clean.

"Well if it isn't our former students," Drone said tonelessly. "Guards, surround that bear. He's dangerous."

Fardels roared a protest, but six bees circled him, their thick, pointed stingers thrust out like swords.

"This disobedient boy," said Drone, waving at me with his heavy walking stick, "is the ringleader. He piloted the blimp. I shall give him the thrashing of his life."

"Really, Drone, *must* you?" objected the queen.

"Indeed I must, Your Majesty. Stand aside!"

"Wait!" shouted Dr. Weedblossom. "I'm the boy's stepfather. Thrash me instead!"

But his offer was ignored.

Lew Ladybug was an angry twitter in front of the headmaster's face. "Listen, Drone," he grated. "Are you itching for a smack in the snoot? You lay one finger on this kid and I'll—"

"You'll *what*?" said Drone with a scornful laugh. "Why, all you are is a puny little big-talking bug. After I finish with the boy, I'll squash you to a smear."

Just then the noonday sun broke through a gap in the clouds. It made me look up. Was I dreaming, or did I see a vast, shadowy bird-shape directly overhead?

My grandfather made a flying leap for Drone's arm, to grab the stick away from him, but two big bees stepped up and captured him. Gramp's brave attempt to save me had distracted Drone for a moment. That was all the time I needed. The prince had given us one more bit of joke equipment—a little round mirror that made your nose look bigger than it was. I held the mirror out flat and caught the shaft of sunlight. Ever so carefully, I tilted the mirror back and forth. The glass gave a dazzling flash. I beamed that flash straight up into the sky.

Drone stepped toward me, his walking stick raised high, looking forward to breaking my head. I had only one weapon. The mirror still clutched in my hand. I flung it at the headmaster with all my might.

The little piece of glass zinged through the air and struck Drone's forehead. And then the darnedest thing happened. Drone's expressionless white face cracked. It completely shattered. Chunks of it fell like snowflakes. It was a beeswax mask. Drone's real head with the five-eyed face of a bee came bursting through.

Parents gasped.

"Yuk!"

"Horrors!"

"What kind of headmaster is *that?*"

Drone gave a furious buzz. He shook off his white wax hands, revealing the two-pronged feet of a bee. "What do I want a mask for? I don't need to look human anymore. Tibb boy, I'm going to thrash you to death—to death, I say!"

But after taking one step toward me, he stopped and heaved a yawn. "On second thought," he mused, "I believe I'll let Xizzix do the thrashing. My arms feel weary from my long, arduous flight."

The Hood stepped forward and Drone passed her the stick.

"Go to work, Xizzix!" said the headmaster. "Finish this boy off!"

Xizzix advanced on me. She moved mechanically, like a robot, holding the stick high over her head. Somehow she looked even scarier than Professor Drone. The stick whistled as she swung it down at me hard.

But the blow didn't land. Three powerful hurricanes came blasting down out of the sky. The first swept Xizzix off her feet, sending the stick skittering. Mademoiselle Stinger was thrown upside down. She landed, and her wax mask split away, too, and her wax hands smashed to bits.

Dimly visible, her vast wings gleaming with wetness, the mother eagle stormed over the lawn, picking up bees and tossing them left and right like a lot of beanbags. I stood there cheering like crazy. Our grandmother was dancing up and down for joy, shouting, "What a battle! Oh, this is spectacular! I'll have to paint a picture of this!"

NOTE BY VERITY: *Thank goodness, the eagles had finished their lunch and had come cruising by, guessing that we might need some help in fighting the bees. When they saw Timmy's signal, they knew just what to do. And they did it.*

Eggbert and Aglet, too, were enjoying themselves. They caught up with Drone and Stinger and hopped on their backs and pinned them both to the ground. You never heard worse language out of a teacher in your life.

With long strides, the mother bird approached Queen Meadea. "You and your miserable schemes!" the eagle shrieked. "Why, you're nothing but an overgrown sac of eggs. I'm going to munch you like a sardine." And she opened and shut her huge beak with a *clack*.

I really thought the queen was done for. But Gramp's calm, even voice rang out, "Stop, Madame Eagle! Spare Her Highness! I have a suggestion for her."

Disappointed, the eagle halted in her tracks. "All right, Eldest Elder, I won't eat her if you say not to. But if she doesn't behave, just turn her over to me. I'll finish her off in two bites."

The queen, looking dejected, waddled up to Gramp and said contritely, "Do with me as you please, Eldest Elder. I was wrong—I let myself be swayed by bad advice. If there is any way I can make amends for the trouble I've caused—"

"Why, Your Majesty," said Gramp kindly, "I suggest that you do what you came here to do. Go, take your workers, and start your brand-new hive. May you rule your second colony more wisely than you ruled your first."

"Oh, I shall," said the queen, sounding sincere. "My workers shall gather nectar from the fields. And I'll tell them not to drink a single drop from the Moonflower."

"And why shouldn't they?" countered Gramp. "The Moonflower is open to every insect—giant bees as well. Its supply of nectar is never-ending. Let your workers drink from it all they like. Your mistake was to want to keep it to yourself."

Right there, in her coronet and golden crown, the queen knelt on the grass before our grandfather. "Forgive me," she said humbly. "You are more merciful than I deserve."

"Rise, if you please, Your Majesty," said Gramp, looking embarrassed. "Not far from this school there's a grove of a thousand immense old oak trees, practically giants, and some of their trunks are hollow. That grove might hold your colony. Lew can show you where it is, can't you, Official Detective?"

"Sure thing, Elder Tibb," said Lew. "I know just the place you mean. Come on, queenie—want to take a look at it?"

"At once!" cried the queen, on her feet again, her wings extended for flight. "This will be a second career for me—a new beginning! My bees and I will become useful citizens of the Land of the Moonflower! You'll see!"

"I'm sure you will," replied Gramp. "There's nothing like bees to make crops and flowers grow. And you giant bees ought to prove hugely valuable."

Eager to begin her new career, the queen with all her bees—except for Drone and Stinger, whom the eagle chicks were still squatting on—buzzed into the air and soared away, following a little red spotted flying dot.

"Now what about this miserable pair?" said the eagle, striding briskly to Drone and Stinger, who squirmed under the eaglets' big flat feet. "They're no good to the new colony. I'll take them back to April Fool Isle and throw 'em back into their old hive. Let nature take its course!"

"No, no, not that!" pleaded Drone.

"Well, what do you expect?" said the eagle. "Don't the other bees always starve you leftover drones? In fact, Professor, you've been lucky. Because you were the queen's advisor, you've lived a whole lot longer than you should."

"What about Mademoiselle Stinger?" asked Verity. "She's a worker bee. She can just go back to her old job, can't she?"

"Indeed she can," said the eagle. "She'll serve out the rest of her days in her old home hive."

To me, that sounded like a lifetime sentence to hard labor, but the mademoiselle murmured her thanks. Gramp didn't raise any objections, so the eagle tossed the two archvillains up onto her back. Then she snatched up Nailkeg and Mumbles.

"And as for these two twerps, they can work for me. I'll need baby-sitters—I'm going to start another family."

"Aw, for crying out loud!" bawled Nailkeg. Mumblehead tried to run. But—*whoosh! whoosh!*—the mother eagle tossed Nailkeg onto Eggbert's back and Mumblehead onto Aglet's. Then with earsplitting shrieks all three half-visible birds roared off into the sky, the wind from their wings flattening everybody below.

"I always knew the kid would end up doing time," said Nailkeg's father with a shrug.

"At last," said Mumblehead's mother, "somebody in this family has an honest job."

The eagles climbed up, up, up in long smooth spirals. When the three of them reached the top of the sky, I saw something amazing. Another vast, half-visible eagle was there to meet them, hovering on glistening wings. I knew who it had to be. The father eagle had returned, looking for his family. A perfect rainbow had appeared, looking big enough to straddle the world. For a long moment the four eagles swooped and circled each other happily, passing to and fro under the rainbow's arch. It must have been a pretty scary ride for their passengers. Then the two parent eagles fell into a flight pattern side by side, heading home with the two chicks flapping after them. I stood there watching until, dried off by the warmth of the sun, they disappeared.

Dr. Weedblossom wrapped an arm around me. "Glad, Tim? About how everything's turned out?"

"Am I ever! Except for one thing. The eagle bit a hole through the little blue blimp's balloon."

"Let's build you another blimp. You can help. And this time, we'll make it fly *fast*."

"School's out," said Verity cheerfully. "Now we don't have any teachers."

"Oh yes you do," said Gramp with a knowing smile.

And picking up Drone's fallen mortarboard hat, he stepped over and fixed it on Ben's head and said, "Congratulations, Headmaster Benjamin Ivy."

Ben looked stunned. "You do me great honor, Eldest Elder Tibb. I—I'm not sure I'm capable."

"Don't be absurd," said our grandmother briskly. "Tim and Verity have told us all about you. You're brave and kind and dutiful, and you know a whole wide world of things."

Everybody cheered. Fardels hoisted our new head-master onto his shoulders and carried him around Ben Ivy School, while all the kids jumped into line behind him in a singing and dancing, skipping and shouting, rock-and-rolling, cartwheeling parade.